A Western Story

A Western Story

Gerald B. Nelson

Illustrated by Robin Lindley

Copyright © 2002 by Gerald B. Nelson.

Library of Congress Number: 2002092696
ISBN: Hardcover   1-4010-6352-7
             Softcover   1-4010-6351-9

All rights reserved. No part of this book may be reproduced or transmitted in any form or by any means, electronic or mechanical, including photocopying, recording, or by any information storage and retrieval system, without permission in writing from the copyright owner.

This is a work of fiction. Names, characters, places and incidents either are the product of the author's imagination or are used fictitiously, and any resemblance to any actual persons, living or dead, events, or locales is entirely coincidental.

This book was printed in the United States of America.

To order additional copies of this book, contact:
Xlibris Corporation
1-888-795-4274
www.Xlibris.com
Orders@Xlibris.com
15659

DEDICATION

To Sandy

The land! don't you feel it? Doesn't it make you want to
go out and lift dead Indians tenderly from their graves,
to steal from them—as if it must be clinging even to
their corpses—some authenticity, that which—
Here not there.

William Carlos Williams.

It's supposed to begin now. My father is dead and buried. I have his diamond-studded Elks Lodge ring in the little leather "wampum" pouch where I carry lucky rocks and the pennies that I have put on railroad tracks. I saw him die; brutally, slowly, unwillingly over a month. Lying in a hospital bed, his mind faded, his body collapsed, leaving only an angry will that hated everything around it. He wanted to get better, but he got worse, drowning in his own fluid—wheezing, gasping—finally they bound his hands in huge bandage mittens so that he couldn't tear at his own body; and, then, I gave them permission to give him morphine. He died gasping for air, his blind eyes staring. I watched him and kept thinking—an awful image flashing through my head—he looks like a fish; a beached fish, dying on the air it had to breathe. I watched his grasping mouth. I knew he was my father and I knew that he was dying, but I kept seeing the fish and biting on the inside of my own cheeks to drive the image away.

But he's dead now. They both are—mother and father. And if I wasn't there to open the door on my mother's body, I was there to shut the door on my father's. His strange son. I was never my brother—he once introduced me as his "son's brother." Neither my brother nor myself was ever what or who he wanted. But, I was there. At the end. And he's dead.

*   *   *

When I got here this morning I had to shoo three cows away from in front of the house. There's nobody around this part of the lake in the winter and the farmer who has the land out back lets his cattle roam free from December until early March. They come down to the lakefront and, if it isn't frozen over solid, they drink and eat the ice-mush. They also leave a lot of cow-pies around which makes the beach a mess in spring.

I drove the cows back up the hill and shouted at them until they headed off towards their pasture. Then I went down and sat on the dock and looked out at the lake before I unpacked my stuff. It's mid-January and usually the North Idaho lakes are frozen by now. Even the big ones like Coeur d'Alene freeze up at least part way out when you get away from the towns. But now the lake is almost clear, just a little broken sheet-ice here and there out about three hundred yards and from that point on it's just dark, shining water. The sun was bright this morning and it made the water look like lovely, green glass.

Oh yes, where. I'm at Coeur d'Alene Lake, about two-thirds of the way down the west shore from the town, where you face the mountains across the lake. My brother used to own the house I came to, but he sold it to a friend a couple of years ago. I kept a key that I had. I came out here without telling anyone. No one comes to this part of the lake in winter. There's no phone and the electricity is cut-off. No one will ever know I'm here. I brought five quarts of vodka; some tonic water, some bread, some salami, some cheese and a bottle of vitamins—I don't want to kill myself.

* * *

"It began with the dead Indian. In Trent Alley, midnight on a Friday, behind the Buck-n-Doe. He was slumped against a wall, the bare-bulb exit light from over the back door of the bar shining on his hat and shoulders. We couldn't see his face. We thought he was drunk and passed out. He smelled terrible. I said something to him—maybe it was "You O.K.?" We were afraid, we were only sixteen and we'd never rolled a drunk Indian before. We'd heard about it in school. Some of the Indians had some money. They weren't all bums. Some of them worked for the railroad, gandy-dancing, and they'd get paid and then blow their money on the fortified wine they could buy in the Indian taverns. The taverns were the only places they could go, the state liquor stores wouldn't even let them in the front doors. We hoped this guy was one of the working ones, and, since it was Friday, that he still had some of his paycheck left. We hoped that nobody else from school—or one of his buddies—had got to him first and rolled him. It was like a Scout Merit badge to roll a drunk Indian and get some money out of it. Even if you didn't need the money. It was a lot better than just beating one up.

Anyway, he didn't answer me. I looked at my friend, Gary. He shrugged his shoulders. I said, "Hey!" I said it again, louder, but not so loud that anybody could hear inside the tavern. There was still no response. Then, Gary reached down and lifted the Indian's hat up. He was just staring out, dead as a doornail. His dead eyes shining in the light from the bare-bulb.

"Christ!"

"What is it?"

"It was terrible. Frightening."

"What did you do?"

"Ran like hell. Right out of the alley. Never looked back and never told anybody about it, either."

"Why not?"

"Tell? Murder. They would have said we killed him. Two years later I really thought about killing a guy, a wino we picked up in Seattle. In Pioneer Square. We drove him out to the Arboretum and dumped him. But we thought about killing him. No reason. Just for . . . "

"Wait a minute. Stick with the Indian. Why would anybody have thought that you killed him? You were just kids. Anyway you didn't even know if he had been killed, did you?"

"No. And he hadn't. In the paper the next day, they had a couple of sentences about him. His liver gave out. He wasn't even a gandy-dancer. He was just a bum. Hell, are you asking me why we ran? We were scared. You tell me. It's like the wino in Seattle. I think I might have killed him—the wino, the Indian, both. No . . . "

Then I was silent for a long time. It was probably only a couple of minutes, but it seemed like an eternity. We were both silent. Just sat there. I was looking at my shoes. I don't know what he was looking at. I picked it up again first. I figured that it was my responsibility. I was paying him for his time. I could still hear my "no" hanging in the air, echoing in my ears.

" . . . I wouldn't have killed them, either one. I don't think I could, really. I mean it's possible, but I can't even kill insects. Maybe I just wanted to hurt them—the Indian and the wino."

"Would you have hurt the Indian . . . if he'd been alive?"

"Moot point, isn't it? I mean I didn't have that decision to make. I don't know."

"Sure you do. You had a plan. When you went down the alley, you had a plan. Maybe even all day you had a plan. Maybe even for a week."

"Or a year?"

"Or a year."

"No plan. I wanted to roll a drunk Indian. Any drunk Indian. Then I could tell people I did—a couple of weeks later I did just that, I made up a story. I told the kids in school, the ones who mattered to me, that I'd gone down to Trent by myself and rolled an Indian. I even showed them an empty pint of fortified apple wine that I found on the street. I told them that I took it from him and poured half of it all over him. No. I didn't have any plan. But, when he didn't answer me, I wanted to hurt him. I wanted to kick him. Even with his dead eyes, I wanted to kick him."

"Why?"

"I don't—no, that's not true. Christ, I feel like I'm hypnotized or something. I can see it. I mean, I can see what I felt then, what I was thinking. I was mad at him. I wanted him to jump up, right up off the ground of the alley. And I wanted all those bum's rags he had on, and that stupid hat to just fall off him. And he'd be wearing a breechclout—like Cochise, or Geronimo, or Joseph, or, best of all, Crazy Horse—and he'd have a tomahawk, or a knife, and we'd fight, right there, in Trent Alley. But it wouldn't be the Alley, it would be the top of Steptoe Butte with a hot sun blazing. And then, somehow, from somewhere, a beautiful

Indian girl would appear and she'd be his sister and she'd be in love with me—because I was a good white man and they were good Indians—and she'd stop the fight. And then we'd be friends and, eventually, I'd marry the girl . . .

God, talk about crazy! You know what happened, really? Another thing I forgot? Gary, my friend, he took the Indian's hat. It was like he was taking a scalp, and he gave it to me and I took it home and hid it in the garage."

I took a deep breath, sighed and shook my head.

"Shit. Some teen-age nut's version of *Broken Arrow*."

"Did you think about Indians a lot when you were young?"

I paused again. Jesus, what a question! After what I'd been trying to say . . . This wasn't an awkward silence because I knew that I had something I wanted to say. I knew what it was. I didn't even care whether he understood it or not. I just wanted to try to get the words right. I wanted to tell the right story.

"I don't know about the Indians. I don't know how to answer what you asked. But I just remembered something that I knew about the history of the West. In the 19th century, I remember that the Army was trying to figure out how to deal with the Indians because they didn't want to give the land up peaceably. One of the ideas that the Army had was to give the Indians contaminated blankets in trade. The blankets had white man's diseases on them and the Indians had no immunity to these diseases, so the Army figured that they could just kill them quietly, just let the bad products of civilization eliminate the threat. Sometimes I think that that's what has happened to the white West. Gradually the East—New York, Boston, Washington, even Chicago—has been shipping all sorts of different diseased, civilized blankets across the plains and the mountains. Even people like me, I go back East and live for twenty years and come back as a blanket. You understand what I mean? I'm not even saying that it's necessarily bad; it's just the way of civilization. Now, so much of what we see out here isn't natural any more, it isn't even healthy, because the West doesn't have any immunity . . . "

"To what?"

"Hell, you name it. Fancy restaurants, the stock market . . . I can't list things. But—well . . . let me try a story. This is true. Maybe it's like the Indian one. It's another kid story. Anyway. When I was thirteen, a friend of mine and I used to take a lot of bike-hikes. We were both in Scouts and we used to head out on Saturday mornings and ride our bikes into the country. Sometimes we'd try to cook out and a couple of times we spent the night in sleeping bags. Well, one time we went way out along the Little Spokane River. We got to a place where even the dirt road ended, so we left our bikes and hiked along the river. It was in August, and hot, so when we got far enough from the end of the road so that we figured that there wouldn't be anybody around, we took off our clothes and went swimming in the river. It was cold in the water, but the river was clean there and we could see the fish at the bottom and actually pretend that the mica glitter on the rocks was gold. We got out of the water and lay down in a field to dry off

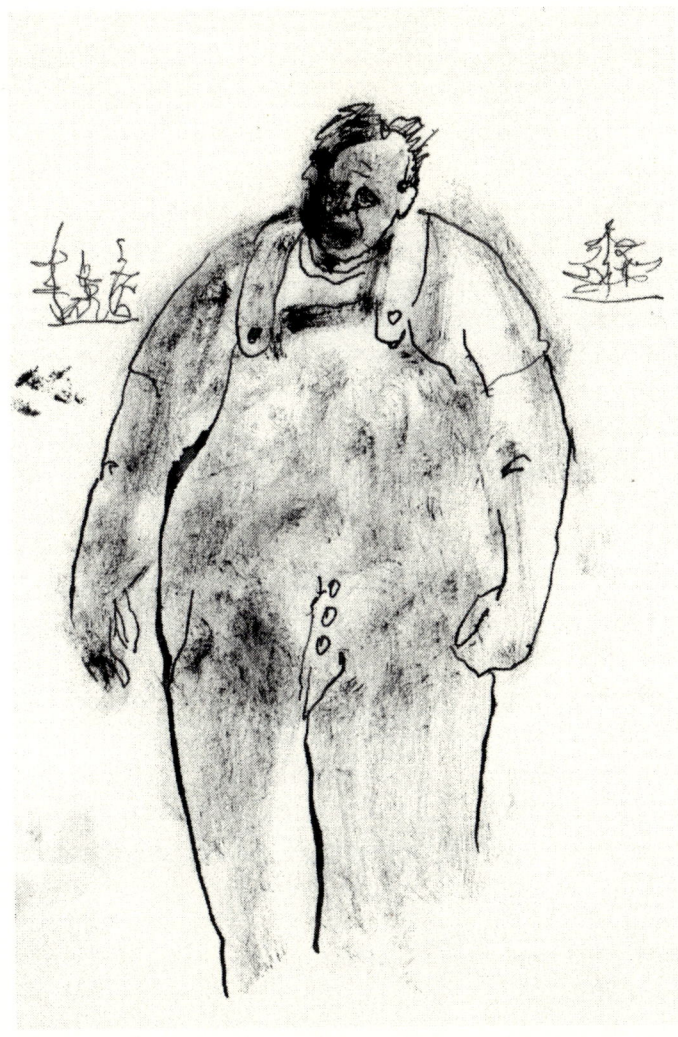

in the sun. We thought the field was wild. But, all of a sudden, while we were lying there squinting up against the sun, a big guy appeared right next to us. He looked enormous, particularly since we were lying on the ground. He was wearing bib-overalls and a flannel work-shirt. Even though it must have been a hundred degrees in the sun. He didn't yell at us. He just squatted down on his haunches next to us. We were trying to cover our nakedness and get up at the same time. This is incredible! I can see him now. He had a little tiny head and it sat, without a neck, on a body that must have weighed two hundred and fifty pounds. He just smiled at us. I was scared to death. I thought he was looking right at my private parts, staring at them. I covered myself with both my hands. He didn't ask us who we were or where we were from. He just grinned. I thought he was a half-wit. Then he said, right out of the blue: "You boys ever had a cow?" I didn't know what he was talking about. My friend tried to answer him. He said something about us being from town and being Scouts. But the guy in the overalls interrupted him. "You know what I mean, don't you, boys? I mean, have you ever fucked a cow?" We hadn't fucked anything. We were even embarrassed to talk about it. "No," my friend stammered. I couldn't say anything. "It's the best," the man in the overalls said. "Better than anything; women, jacking-off, anything you name. Cow is so damn big and then it looks around at you with those eyes and it's just like it was smiling at you; just like it was in love with you." He smiled a big grin at us, showing all sorts of broken teeth. His eyes were tearing. "It's the best thing in the world. Just you boys remember that." Then he got up off his haunches. He didn't touch us and he didn't say anything else. He just shook his head back and forth, grinning that big grin. Then he turned away and shambled off across the field and into the trees. My friend and I looked at each other. We didn't laugh. We weren't scared anymore. We just felt nervous. And dirty. We ran across the field and jumped back into the cold river water.

Later on—six years later—I met two guys in college. One of them was a farm kid and the other pretended to be—like me he had an uncle who had a farm—and they got into a discussion that turned into a fierce argument over which was best: A sheep or a cow. The kid whose uncle owned a farm argued for the sheep. He was smarter than the other kid and I thought that he won the argument. He acted like a debater and claimed that the sheep was more responsive because it was more intelligent; it knew what it was doing, so there were grounds for believing that true romance was possible. He ended up a doctor—a brain surgeon."

I stopped and looked hard at him. "You see what I mean?"

"About what?"

"About the West."

* * *

I don't know what this is. Maybe it's just a way to start talking. Therapy and I . . . well, just let it go at this. Maybe what I just talked about was said with someone else in the room; maybe I was paying him; maybe it was just me; maybe it doesn't make any difference to anybody but me; and maybe I need to stop this first day and go out to the edge of the water and see if I can smell the moon.

The telephone woke me from the dream. My wife answered it and I grumbled about not wanting to get up and take over for Amalia and drive her daughter and mine to nursery school. I did it too much; it wasn't really my chore; plus, I'd been up drinking by myself until four in the morning. It was six and the call was long distance. My wife handed the phone to me and mouthed the words "Your mother's dead."

She was, suddenly, totally unexpectedly. I had talked to her a week before, from my house in Long

Island to my parents' winter place in Palm Desert and she had been fine—oh, she had thought that maybe she was getting the flu. My father was talking to me, telling me. Crazy, sobbing, desperate bastard. He was talking about himself, getting himself off the hook, wanting me to pity him. She had gotten up in the middle of the night and gone into the bathroom, he had gone back to sleep. When he woke up and she wasn't in bed he called for her—probably demanding his breakfast—and when she didn't answer he went into the bathroom. There she was, sitting on the toilet. She had exploded, a terrible cancerous blast of tumor in her bowels. I never knew more detail than that. Just her, dead, on the toilet. But, oh God, what images I have made in my mind over the years: My mother's beautiful face—and then the nightmare of what must have been on that bathroom floor. When my father told me my mind went crazy. I blamed him. Somehow, I knew, his failures, the sloth of his wasted later years were responsible, and yet I shuddered with him and for him as I tried to imagine the shock, the horror of what he must have seen. Even though it's just a few words of his and my image, I still can't bring myself to really imagine seeing it.

My brother was there, staying in the desert with his family, close to my parents' place. He would handle the details. All I had to do was get myself to Seattle where they would ship the body for the funeral.

This is very bad. I've got part of the image of my mother's body in my mind. But I can't look at her face. I can see her feet and water all around them on the tiles of the floor, and the side of the bathtub, and the bottom of her robe and the fluffy slippers she used to wear, and then I start to stare, to try to focus all my attention on the damn towel rack that was next to the toilet in their Palm Desert place, and I see the towels all neatly folded over the bars of the rack. But, I can't look at her face—because it isn't her!

Jesus! I have to walk it down in my mind.

By the time I got on the plane for Seattle the next day, I had barely slept and had been drinking and popping Valium steadily. Before I boarded I took an extra five 5mg. tab of Valium and had six double vodka and tonics in the airport. Yet my nerves were keeping me so straight that I could hardly stand it. I was terrified of flying—vertigo, claustrophobia—and, at the time I had a horrible prescience of doom.

I sat next to a soldier who was coming home from Vietnam. I drank drink after drink. Someplace just before the Rockies, a young guy who was sitting towards the front of the plane jumped up and started yelling about the emergency exit. "Let me out!" he screamed. "We're going to crash! We're going to die! Let me out!" The soldier turned to me and said, "That guy's crazy." I said, "He may be crazy, but he's right, and if he can find that exit door, I'm going with him." There was a doctor on the plane who gave the screamer a shot and the soldier didn't speak to me the rest of the trip.

At my mother's funeral I knew, drunk as I was, that the world had died. I tried to take care of my father; it was almost as though I loved him. My aunts all kissed the corpse in the coffin; I could barely look at it—it was plastic, frozen, a model of my mother, not her. The minister asked the assembled what we wanted done with the flowers, I got up and ran up the aisle and yelled, "We don't want them! Give them to my aunts!" Afterwards, at the family "party," my Jesus-jumping, John Birch uncle stared at my beard and long hair and called me a "Commie," he told me that I had some nerve showing myself at a family funeral; my sweet cousin Jean told me: "Your mother isn't really gone, you know. It's just like she's on a trip. Imagine her in Paris. You'll see her again." I said: "Jean, she's dead. This joke's over." One of my aunts and my sister-in-law told me that they were afraid that I had lost control. I had.

When my father died my brother was at Disneyland with his children and grandchildren. I couldn't tell him until the next day.

After my mother's funeral I decided that I couldn't fly back East. I wanted to feel the land across the country. I stayed in Seattle an extra week and then I took the train; the Great Northern Empire Builder, the same train I used to ride between Seattle and Spokane with my mother when I was a kid. The first night on the train I sat in the club car. I talked to two people: One was a woman in her late thirties; she was badly drunk and acted very sexy towards me. She was going to Montana; her husband was in a coffin in the baggage car. He had died just as they were getting ready to board a flight to Hawaii. The other person I talked with was a soldier. He was going to North Dakota. He had met his brother's remains in Seattle and was ushering them home for burial. His brother had been a soldier too. He had been killed in Vietnam. After that night, I drank in my roomette. I didn't talk to anybody else, except the porters.

Anger or self-pity, which comes first? Which is worse? It really is better to be alone.

When I got back East, it was all different. I didn't go back to teaching for a month. I drank. I ran around, bar to bar, going to those low-life Italian cocktail lounges that are all over Long Island. When

I did go back to teaching, I didn't want to teach English literature anymore. I wanted to teach American literature. But it wasn't the literature I was really interested in. I didn't so much want students to know what Melville or Poe or Hawthorne thought as I wanted them to know what I thought the writers were saying—about America; and what I told the students that Melville or the others were saying was what I was thinking. I wanted desperately to be an American. But not an American living in a city. I wanted to be and I wanted the writers and the students to be what I had so wanted my grandfather and my father to be: Frontiersmen, that's what I wanted. I wanted Hawthorne to be a frontiersman, not a scared little man hiding in his room afraid of the woods like his character Arthur Dimmesdale. I wanted to see him lie down with some real-life Hester Prynne and make love with her in a clearing in the wilderness while a whole tribe of Indians, covered with paint made out of barks and roots, danced around them in May-Day circles.

I wanted to be my grandfather. I wanted to be what my image of my grandfather was before I was born and got to know him as an old man who took care of cattle and talked to his ten year old grandson about finding—the two of them setting off and trekking through the wilds—the Northwest Passage. He died two months before my mother did. He was almost one hundred and three and he died in his sleep. When my mother called to tell me the news of his death, all I said was something to the effect that he had "lived a long life." A very stupid thing to say and not at all what I meant.

But, if I wanted to be him, I never outright told anybody so. Instead I started talking a lot about

Indians. I talked about blankets and about the way the white man took the land. I read my students Chief Sealth's speech about the spirits remaining in the land—the spirits of the dead Indians—and how they would haunt the white man even through the pavements of his city streets. I told my students to listen for the cries of Indians as they got on buses, to strain their ears for the strange tongues hidden in the roar of the subways. And I would be an Indian in my classroom, I would honor the four directions, the sky, the earth, show them the drum beat in the blood and walk Indian paths around them in the lecture hall; or I would lecture to two hundred and fifty people about *Moby-Dick* and I would be Ahab, thumping on a make-believe peg up and down the aisles, circling the class shouting warnings like Father Mapple. A prophet of doom, who took the madness of Thoreau in the woods of Maine and made an act of it—sugar-coating my venomous pills with the trappings of entertainment. On and on. I chased my America like a dog chasing his tail.

Then one day a black teacher came to my office. I knew about him by reputation and I thought him to be a hustler and a con man; a soul-less, self-serving fool—the kind of man who took "credit to your race" as a compliment. He came to me with a proposition. "You," he said, "have quite a reputation as a radical. And I hear that you're doing work with Indians. I'm in the history department and I'm interested in Indians, too, so perhaps you might be interested in doing a course with me, inter-disciplinary, on America and the Indians. You know: Literature and history, sociology . . . " I'm probably not quoting him right. I know that I'm not conveying the tone of his words, so I'll at least try to be true in reporting my response to him. I said: "You've heard about me. I've heard about you. Let me translate the euphemisms, the delicate bureaucratese that you just used, so that we can really understand each other. All right? You have heard that I have two hundred and up in my classes and you like those figures. You figure that if a white man talking about Indians is good for numbers like that, that a salt and pepper team doing the same thing could double the total and you could cut yourself a nice free ride. 'Literature and history.' Right? Well, I don't read or speak Indian languages and you don't either. About the only thing I do know is that it may be best, since I've called you out from under your rock, to leave the Indians alone for awhile. You've helped me come to that decision. That we've done together. I think that we both have enough trouble with our 'own kind.' God knows I have enough with whites, and I suppose it can't be easy being black either."

I hope I'm quoting myself right. At least it was something very like that. The spirit's right.

After that I got crazy in a way that lost its substance. I talked to my teaching assistants about having snipers in the back of the lecture hall; about what it would be like; about how American it would be to have guys like the one who sat on the tower down in Texas hidden up in the projection booth at the back of the balcony just popping off students at the nod of one of our heads. There were older people in my big lectures, people from town. There was a nun. One time I screamed at her. "Sister," I yelled—I was supposedly talking about the book, *Wise Blood* by the Catholic writer, Flannery O'Connor—"Where is Jesus in America, Sister?"

Then I slowed down. The doorman at my mother-in-law's apartment building on Park Avenue in New York found me crawling around on my hands and knees on the sidewalk in front of the building. They wanted to put me in Bellevue. Instead, I ended up in a hospital on Long Island where I set a hospital record for Thorazine. But that leads to another story.

And I want to talk about, to see my grandfather in my mind. My mother's father. I don't know if I ever really thought about him until after my mother died. My father always said that he was a crazy man; a worthless dreamer.

He was born in the last year of the Civil War. He died right after Richard Nixon was elected President. It used to amaze me when I looked at him after I was an adult and he was a very old man that he had grown up before there was electricity or automobiles. There he was in the age of airplanes, atom bombs and moon-shots and he had known the railroad train as a miracle of science.

I don't know anything about his childhood and much of what I know about his life is all mixed up with family stories and what I want to make of him as a sort of myth.

He worked in the mills in Pennsylvania, as a laborer, and somehow he picked up the skills of a carpenter. He was married twice. His first wife died young and he had all his children with my grandmother. They were all born—the six children—in Pennsylvania. His story could have stopped there and he would have been just another turn-of-the-century mill-worker in the industrial East, but something happened to him, something cracked a little bit and what my father called "the dreamer" put down his lunch sack and the pail of beer that my aunt used to carry to him at the mill and headed West.

He had a brother—who I never met—and they got together and gave themselves nicknames: Ripsaw Joe for my grandfather and Hand-axe Pete for his brother. They left their families—temporarily—and went out to the new park in Montana, called

Glacier, and got themselves jobs as carpenters building lodges for the tourists that the government knew the railroads would bring to see the remains of the American Wilderness.

    Along with building parks, the government was also giving away Montana land at that time; parcels of what the railroad speculators and the city-builders claimed was "farmable" land. The government called them Homesteads, and anyone could have his own personal parcel if he promised to work and improve the land. My grandfather took his, a section that he figured might not be too arid or desolate because it had a stream running along one edge. He didn't know that the stream wasn't a real and permanent river, that it was just a large rivulet of run-off from the spring snow-melt in the higher ground—it ran wet for less than a month a year. He sent East for his family. My grandmother and her six children got on a train in Pennsylvania and went across the country jammed in with hundreds of other wives and children of Montana Dreamers. They saw the Mississippi and then, a little past the Missouri, they got off the train and there were a few stores and saloons and horses and some motorcars and they were in Great Falls, Montana.

    They lived there for nine years, fighting the weather and the land, in a two-room house where the kids slept two to a bed and shared the winter clothes. In later times, when all the kids had grown old themselves, they used to talk about life on the "ranch" as the happiest time of their lives. Even as a child I wondered how that could be true.

    They left the ranch because my grandfather went to Portland, Oregon on one of his periodic wanderings. He played pinochle with a Chinese— he used to warn me over and over when I was little about "pinochle with the Chinks;" and used to chant a little song, it went: "Chink, Chink, Chinaman / Sitting on a fence / Trying to make a dollar / Out of fifteen cents"—and when the pinochle game was over he had swapped his homestead in Montana to the Chinese for a donut recipe and a piece of land. Sight unseen. The land turned out to be on a mountaintop outside of Bellingham, almost at the Canadian border. Members of my family know where it is, but nobody has ever been there.

Nothing happened with the donut recipe, but the whole family moved to Seattle, and my grandfather worked odd jobs as a carpenter for a while. Then he worked steadily, but he was in his sixties and he was content to just build things and be the first man on the job in the morning where he would make coffee for the rest of the crew—his own special coffee, with crushed up egg-shells in it—and it would be ready for them when they got to work. By this time it was the 1930s and Seattle was becoming a hustling, modern, twentieth century city, but his bosses and the men he worked with, all of whom were much younger than he, thought that my grandfather with his dawn coffee, his stories and the way he worked must have somehow secretly believed that he and the men were building towns on the frontier, carving away at the wilderness; telling tales in whispers and working fast so as not to alert the Indians.

During the Second World War, he was in his late seventies. He lied about his age so that he could work on the docks in Seattle—stevedore work, loading.

After the war, he started helping my uncle. My uncle had a city job, but longed for the country. He bought a broken down farm north of Seattle and my grandfather built him a barn and then my grandfather started raising cows—not cattle, cows—and he bought a horse and then another one, and a whole coop of bantie chickens.

I loved to stay at my uncle's farm. My parents started leaving me with my uncle and aunt for six weeks or so in the summer when I was nine years old. They went off to do other things, mainly to go to Elks Conventions. So, I was "farmed out." I didn't do any chores. There really weren't any. There was a little vegetable garden; and there was my grandfather with his pet cows and horses and chickens. He scared me then, because I couldn't understand what he would say to me. When we would go off together, and I would watch as he cut down a sapling or cleared brush in the wild land bordering the farm, he would talk to me, or, maybe it wasn't to me as much as it was to himself—no, no, that's wrong; it was to me, but I was from a different world and he didn't realize it. He would talk to me about Indians; about how he had Indian blood—Cherokee—in him, so that he knew you could trust the Indians, but not the Chinamen, the damn Chinamen! An Indian was like a tree in the woods, but a Chinaman was like a dog—somebody had brought him and dumped him in the woods and the only thing he knew was to cheat his way out. And he would talk about the Northwest Passage, the single waterway across the whole of the continent. He knew it was there—the Indian in him told him so—and he and I would find it and be rich men; a man in his eighties and a boy of nine or ten.

I made him furious at me the second summer I stayed at the farm. He had put one of his bantie hens and a whole brood of newly hatched chicks in a big cardboard box so that they would be safe. The box had a lid on it so that cats or wild birds couldn't get in and hurt the chicks. I took one of the semi-wild outdoor cats that lived on the farm and dropped it into the box. Then I shut the lid and made my six-year-old girl cousin sit on it. There were terrible noises from inside the box and it shook and almost buckled. When it quieted down, my cousin jumped off and we opened the lid. The cat jumped out and took off. All the chicks and the mother were dead and there was blood all over the inside of the box.

I don't know why I did it.

That's not true. I know why all right.

But I want to hold on to a picture of my grandfather that I have in my mind. The one of him looking up from the tree he has cut down and gesturing with his axe, pointing north into the woods, with a bright-eyed sweaty smile on his face. Later on he got a little crazier.

* * *

I walked up on the hill behind the cabin last night. Up to the top. It's all woods. The farmer's land doesn't begin until the hill dips down into a steep valley. There wasn't any moon at all, so it was pure dark. I could smell the pines and the strong, biting scent of the firs, and I could feel my way through the forest with my hands. It was nasty cold, but I still sat down and took my shoes and socks off and hung them around my neck. I wanted to feel everything I could and I wanted to hear the silence of the woods. I thought of the Donner Party.

* * *

I've read books where Indians and Negroes are

compared. Not sociology books, or quasi-biology books where the differences and similarities between races are talked about, but those dark, revisionist history or literary criticism books about the American Experience. In them, concerned guys with reputable PhDs talk about how our forefathers' terrible fear of the strange red man they found in the forests of America caused them to buy, train and breed another, darker breed of man who would serve them if they neutered him. The arguments of these authors all revolved about the fear of the strange and different that the English lower middle-class found on the new continent. Different animals, different birds, different trees and different people—all, because they were different, dangerous. They found a whole world that had to be named anew and then tamed, or eliminated. We had to kill the Indian because he was untamable, so we brought the Negro to replace him as a creature we could both fear and control.

A lot of times books that talk about things like that make sense to me.

Sometimes I think that I can't stop talking or thinking about Indians, it seems they haunt me—no, no, it's not some sort of white "liberal guilt," at least I hope not. I don't hear their voices through the pavement, and, no, I don't really believe my grandfather's claim about the Cherokee blood—I think about them; I think about the way they looked to me when I was a child. Going down to Main or Trent in Spokane where you could see them was like going to a sideshow at a circus.

They used to have paintings of the great Indian chiefs in the dining cars of the Great Northern Empire Builder trains. When my mother and I would take the day train to Seattle, we would always have lunch in the dining car and I would always ask one of the Negro porters to explain who the Indian chiefs were—I was very young then, three, four, five and the porters were always huge, dressed in blazing white and gold, and very, very black; it's a dim memory, save for the porters—the porter would always smile and tell me to ask my "Mommy."

The way I remember the Indians around Trent and Main and the railroad tracks in Spokane is much different from the craggy-faced color paintings of the Great Chiefs in all their feathers and colors. The Indians on the street have blended into MY PICTURE that I carry in my head: A Breugel, maybe—the blind leading the blind—updated into the twentieth century; red men in rags and torn hats lying on the streets, or staggering around, or leaning, helpless, against the walls of buildings, while well-dressed, erect white men, women and children pass among them oblivious to the madness of the scene surrounding them. I don't know if that's clear or not. Maybe . . . try a Walt Disney movie that mixes live actors with cartoon characters, with the whites as the live actors and the Indians as the cartoon characters; the two species can look at one another and even touch, but all the time you know that one is real and the other make-believe.

All that is by way of saying that Indians, by the time that I knew them weren't real anymore, at least in Spokane. They were curiosities, depressing curiosities, but still just broken souvenirs from the past. Town Indians, which were all I ever saw, were off the Reservation and hence off the government payroll. They gandy-danced or got menial jobs cleaning rest rooms in train stations or saloons.

Sometimes they would just odd job for wine money. Everybody said they were drunk all the time. If they fought it was only with each other. The town treated them like unwanted, deserted mongrel dogs.

I was taught to pity and avoid them, as though their decay were contagious.

One day, when I was six, I came home from school chanting "Eeny, Meeny, Miny, Moe / Catch a Nigger by the toe / If he hollers let him go / Eeny, Meeny, Miny, Moe." My mother grabbed me by both shoulders and looked hard into my face. "Don't ever say that around them," she said. "If you do and they hear you, they'll kill you." The only "niggers" I had seen were the porters on the Great Northern and the waiters and waitresses in the Coon Chicken Inn—which was a restaurant on Lake City Way in Seattle that I went to with all my aunts and uncles and cousins. The building was a huge, open-mouthed, grinning black head with a giant chef's cap; you walked into the restaurant over the carpet of a tongue, between ruby red lips and brilliant-white gigantic teeth—and the vision of a black man in a white suit, or bouncy black kids in waiter's clothes hurting me so badly that I died—which I couldn't really understand—or the mouth of the Coon Chicken Inn clamping down on me and my whole family and crushing us between those enormous teeth, flashed in pure terror through my mind.

What I'm trying to say is that when I was very little what I felt when I looked at Indians, Negroes or Asians was a sense of wonder at the difference, the difference in color and the way their faces were shaped—and that sense of wonder was a close brood-brother of fear. And the more I was told by way of explanation of the differences, the more afraid I became until I think that I turned into a twentieth century model of one of the more timid kids in the early settlements of Pennsylvania or Ohio—terrified of the woods because of the strange red creatures that lurked there with murder in their hearts. Except for me the woods were the streets of my hometown.

Is that Western enough for you?

My contact with "different" kids while I was growing up was limited, almost as though God or Fate or something had selected random incidents and people to stand as object lessons for young, white me. There was Gail, a Japanese girl I met in the sixth grade. She came to my school when her family was released from the internment camp. The only other Japanese I'd ever seen had been on the screen; the ones who killed Brian Donlevy in *Wake Island*, or tortured Dana Andrews and Farley Granger to death in *The Purple Heart*—they were Japs. And I used to kill Japs myself. My brother gave me some old, metal toy soldiers and I would use them to create my own battles, where my heroes with names like the Creeper and the Crawler would infiltrate Jap camps and kill hundreds of the enemy in brutal single-hand combat. I made sure that there were no *Wake Island* disasters in my imagination.

I sat next to Gail in the classroom and she smelled very soapy and clean. She wore new clothes and she would smile at me when she caught me staring at her. I couldn't help myself in the staring. Her eyes looked so funny and her nose was all flat and the color of her skin was tanner than my farm-aunt's arms in the summer. She wasn't bright yellow like I had expected.

When she opened up enough to tell me that she'd been in camp, I said: "That's neat. I didn't know you got to go to camp. I thought you all went to jail."

When I was in the seventh grade, I played basketball with a boy named Sid. I thought he was pretty neat so I asked him to come home with me after practice one day and watch some eight-millimeter cartoons on our movie projector. My father came home and found Sid there and ordered him out of the house. The next day my father took me on a drive downtown and pointed out the pawnshops and cut-rate clothing stores along Riverside and Main. "Jews own those," he said. "I don't want Jews in my house. They'll cheat the pants off you—take your money; steal you blind." I didn't meet another Jew until college. I brought two Jewish friends home. My father said nothing; my mother simply asked: "They're Jews, aren't they?"

My first wife is Jewish. My father started screaming over the phone when I told him about the marriage; my mother was conciliatory. "It's not so bad, dear," she said to my father over the extension phone, "he could have married a Negro."

Indians, of course, were easy—if you don't count thinking.

But Negroes. There was a black kid named Louie who transferred from across town to go to my high school. We had other black students at Lewis and Clark, but it seemed that they were all functionaries, interchangeable. No black girls. Just, it seems, one black male per year and he played halfback in football; was elected to the meaningless fifth executive's position in the Boy's Fed organization; and had a good enough voice to sing "Old Man River" at the Minstrel Show Assembly. Louie was different. He was big and slouchy-mean-looking. He had his hair long and pomaded. He hung out with white kids, even danced with white girls at The Spot. Every guy was terrified of him and would try to show off for him, try to show him how tough they were; that they were mean enough to be his buddies. All Louie would ever do was to smile a sort of smirk.

Once when my parents were out of town for a long time, Louie ended up at my house after a party. I thought I was pretty much in control of things at the time. I was "one of the boys" only more so because I was smarter—if we'd used words like "liberated" in the early fifties, I would have thought that I was "liberated" but too "cool" to talk about it. I told Louie to stay at my house. He did—for a week, eating like a horse and sitting on the front porch in the afternoon. He slept in my parents' bed. I tried to act as though I were . . . well . . . "liberated" . . . and would laugh with my friends about what my parents would say when they got home and heard from the neighbors that a nigger had been sitting on their front steps the whole time they were gone.

Mostly, I was terrified. I didn't want Louie in the house. I didn't want him using our sheets, our dishes, even our toilet. I thought his black would rub off on things. I would go out every night and stay out as late as I could. I didn't come home after school. I gave the house to him. I knew that if I tried to take him back to his house that he would kill me. And I was sure that he could read my mind, or, even if he couldn't, he just might decide to kill me for the fun of it. Finally, my friend Gary and I—and I don't remember how we found the courage to do it—got him into my car and took him home. He lived way out on the northeast side of town, next to the railroad freight sidings. When he got out of the car, he said: "Thanks a lot."

Later that same year, Gary and two other guys and myself got drunk and got a cab driver to take us to a Negro whore-house, down in the old Coontown below the hospitals and the big Episcopal Cathedral. We were all scared as hell, and only Gary and I "bought," the other guys shot craps against a living room wall with the cabby and some other black guy. Gary went into a bedroom with a tiny consumptive who was almost a light gray in color, and I took the other woman. She was huge, maybe two hundred pounds and jet-black. She went into the bedroom and turned off the light. I could hear the rustle of clothes but I couldn't see anything. I knew that I could never get a hard-on, maybe really never. She said: "Come on!" in a big, throaty rumble. "I can't see you," I said. "You'll find me, white boy. That little pecker you got's gonna show you the way." She laughed and I saw the flash of her teeth. I got undressed and staggered on top of her. I don't think that I got inside of her. I could smell the perfume and the bedclothes and I was dizzy. I came and she roared and laughed and pushed me off of her. She grabbed a robe and burst through the door, flooding the room with light from the living room. The other two guys who were with us were sitting on a couch facing the open door. I tried to cover myself up with a bedspread. "He came with a softy!" She roared, laughing, spitting and coughing all at the same time, "He came with a softy!"

The next day I went down to see our family

doctor, to get a shot of penicillin. I was terrified of clap. "I kissed a girl last night," I told him, "and I don't think she was very clean." He just smiled at me and I looked at all the pictures of the different happy families that represented his happy practice that were arrayed over his shoulder on the bookcase. Two years before he had scarred my face with misdiagnosed ultraviolet treatments for acne—and five years later he would fuck my mother up forever with mistreatment—but he was the only doctor I knew, and clap and syph were punishments I knew I didn't deserve for my sin. "The nurse will give you a shot," he said, still smiling that secure smile.

One more thing about Negroes. The night before I was to leave Spokane to start my freshman year in college, two friends of mine and I bought two cases of beer. I could buy beer without ID because I looked older—at least that's what I thought. There was a big party that night, a gathering of all the kids who were going to go to college. We decided to drink some beer by ourselves before we went to the party, so we drove down by the Little Spokane River and parked on an old road under the railroad bridge that everybody called High Bridge. We'd had about two beers apiece, when a cop car pulled up out of nowhere behind us. The cops were tough. We were scared. We were going to college; we couldn't afford to get into trouble. We offered them the beer. They laughed at us and split us up. They took my friend John in the squad car, and one of the cops drove my car, with me in the front seat and my friend Frank in the back. They wanted to know how we got the beer. I wanted to stay out of worse trouble and I needed somebody to blame, somebody to scapegoat. So I told them a huge, rambling lie. "We got it from a Negro," I said, "a tall, thin Negro. He was wearing a powder blue, one-button-roll suit, a Mr. B. collar shirt, a black string tie . . . " on and on. Luckily, in the squad car, John was not being specific. He only told the other cop that we got it—I got it—from a Negro and John hadn't even seen the Negro.

I told them the bar where the Negro bought it; down on First, east of Division (close by the whorehouse). It was an all-black bar. The cops rendezvoused back at the station. They left my car there and the two cops and the three of us went to the bar on First to find the imaginary Negro who had sold me the beer. The squad car pulled up in front of the bar, and the cops sent me in alone. I was the only white in the place and every black face showed that it knew precisely why I was there. It was silent and I pretended to look around. I knew that I would die. Then one of the cops came in and talked to the bartender. The cop pointed at me and the bartender started to laugh. "He's lying. Ain't no fool around here dresses like that. That's just some scared, crazy white boy you got there!" He was laughing and shouting, and soon everybody else in the place was laughing, too. Looking at me and laughing. Even the cop had to start to smile. "You tell me, officer, you ever hear of a self-respecting nigger who would dress himself up like a clown?"

But, you know something? Still, deep in my mind I know that if that cop hadn't been in there, that they wouldn't have been laughing and that I would be dead right now. I know that.

I think my mother was wrong. I don't think I could have married a Negro.

* * *

Early this morning I went down to the dock and sat on the end of it and looked out over the lake. Directly across, coming out of the entrance of the St. Joe River, there's a big flotilla of logs—a two-boom mass of fresh cut timber. It wasn't moving so I guess that it's there to stay through the winter. Am I? In the early spring tugs will come out from Coeur d'Alene town and move the logs down to the mill. I know that a rescue party came for the Donner Party, too, but they found Keseberg, glassy-eyed, eating Tamsen Donner's lungs and grinning.

I didn't sleep very well again last night. It was warm enough. The wood stove heats the whole cabin. But I get the bad nighttime frights. It's either too much vodka or not enough. I'm never sure any more. Probably it's not enough; too much and I'd pass out and then wake up with hallucinations and beginning withdrawal. I'm watching out for that. I said I don't want to kill myself, so I'm being careful with the vodka. Just enough to keep one step ahead of bad angst. I want to be rational; I want to remember, to be able to think things out. This time around I don't want the screaming. I don't want to lie down in the bathtub with a kitchen knife. I don't want someone to find me and feel sorry for me. So, I'm being careful.

I really don't want to dull myself. But trying to walk that thin line is very difficult. I want the vodka to obey me, not the other way around. I want it to

help me not control me. Just enough to open the gates in my mind, not so much that I see my father risen from the dead. I'm smart enough—still—to realize that it's a losing battle; that I'm just bargaining with my own Satan for a little time, just time enough to think a bit. Talk to myself. I know the vodka will get me in the end. It always does.

In the meantime, while fighting the battle, one of the things I have to sacrifice is sleep. I get a little, but mostly the dark hours are just lying in my sleeping bag and shaking slightly all over—neural itches that I can't scratch. When I was a little kid and couldn't sleep because I was upset about something that had happened to me, I would think about Mickey Mouse—Disney cartoons—and it would calm me, kind of like telling myself happy stories. Now, lying in the dark, quivering, with just enough alcohol in my system to maintain balance, I think about the things that made me think about Mickey Mouse so long ago in my past.

Down at the dock this morning, while I was looking at the log booms across the lake, I started to think about Dr. Howard Shumsky.

In order to get out of the hospital on Long Island—the one I was put in when I was found crawling around on my hands and knees on the Park Avenue sidewalk; the one where they filled me with Thorazine to get me off Valium and—briefly—alcohol—I had to agree to see a psychiatrist. I don't remember clearly whether I actually had to agree in order to get out—I think that sort of thing is illegal—but the doctor who had my case was a mean, hard-line man. He told me that if I ever drank again and came to his office to ask for help that he would lock the door on me.

Whatever. He told me that I had to see a psychiatrist. He also told me that I was killing my family along with myself. He might just as well have told me that I was killing the world. I met one psychiatrist in the hospital and he was so cold he scared me. So, blind, never having met the man, I agreed to go to Howard Shumsky.

Shumsky and I never talked about drinking. After seeing him twice a week for a month, I started drinking again. It got worse and worse until, eventually, I settled into a routine. I would drink enough before I saw him to enable me to relax and believe that I was in control of the session. I drank vodka out of soda pop cans in his parking lot, and then, sitting in his office with dark glasses on, I would tell him about dreams of my mother still being alive, or about my difficulties in teaching, and he would tell me what a nice guy I was. Never, never did we mention that my marriage was a disaster or that I was a drunk. Like the old, bad play: There was "something unspoken" between us.

One thing stands out in what passed for my therapy. I felt that I should have a physical—I was badly afraid of cirrhosis—and he gave me the names of two doctors and said: "You pick." I did and went to one of the doctors. He was a black man. He told me that my heart and liver were O.K., but that I weighed three hundred pounds and should watch my weight. I went back to Shumsky. He smiled at me and said: "It was a little test. I had begun to wonder if you were racially prejudiced . . . just some of the things you have said lately."

You know why I'm so bitter about Shumsky? It's because I can't figure out why he didn't even try to help me. Something in me must have been crying out. You'd think that he should have been able to hear it! Even if he didn't like me, you'd think that he would have tried to help, or, at least, felt bound by some sort of honor to have told me to go somewhere else. When I finally stopped going to him, I felt that there was no place to go. That's why I'm here, out alone at this lake in the middle of winter. I still feel that there is no place to go. Except home. Except somewhere inside of myself.

My father used to say that no one in our family could ever go to a psychiatrist. It was unthinkable. An admission of terrible weakness.

But, then, he used to feel that even saying, "I love you," was somehow a confession of frailty of the spirit. He said that we were all doers—we had to be—not dreamers. He used himself as an example: The son of illiterate immigrants who worked his way through high school and to the top of Spokane business, to the Manito Golf Club, to the Elks Lodge. But what did it get him? He ended up miserable, old, blind, alone . . . dead.

He was a bad drunk. He got drunk on the road, hustling insurance policies on Indian Reservations and in Lumber Camps—getting drunk with the Chiefs and the loggers, who turned out to be foremen, and, eventually, owners. He met people in the woods and in the tank towns of the West. They were people like him: Smart, uneducated, scornful of weakness, and, as the forests fell and the tank towns filled with money, they grew through their strength and endurance and he grew along with them. They were native frogs in huge natural ponds. They knew the land. They owned it. Loggers, truckers—they were like the Indians.

And then the East bought them out, and my father found himself, saying "ain't" and "them guys" in board rooms of newly formed conglomerates, trying to peddle his home-grown, small-town brand of "man-to-man" insurance in competition with whole squads of three-piece-suited, ivy-educated "gentlemen" from the East. And, in those rooms, his only ally would be the old drunk original logger or trucker he had shared a pint with in a camp in the woods, and that "original" would be nothing more than a silent, numbed presence of authenticity in the room, sitting alone against a far wall, and my father would be overwhelmed by the enormity of the thing he had sold out to.

And my father would come back from those meetings, driving thousands of miles in his Lincoln, with huge hunks of his spirit torn away.

Then he stopped drinking. Then he stopped working. And he would sit in his bathrobe and watch television and my mother would bring him his meals on TV trays and he would go to bed at seven o'clock at night. And then my mother died and he was left alone without his loggers, his truckers or his Indians.

* * *

What am I trying to accomplish with these notebooks, writing things about my life and my family history in the harsh, bright winter light of the lakeshore? Or, am I really writing this all down? Am I talking to myself? Do I want some kind of absolution? Some kind of ordering that will enable me to bury the past and move on into whatever the future is? Or, am I just whining to myself in the woods, hoping to hell nobody else ever hears this cheap self-pitying trash? Who cares what I think about Indians, or Negroes, for god's sake? Who would even care who I am, or was? Keseberg would know. Wait awhile and I'm a piece of meat.

When I was young, I had a feeling, near to a certainty, that writing something down made it real; that putting a hope or a resolution, or telling a story in words on paper gave it legitimacy. My mother taught me to read and write before I started school.

I think she did it, because, at the age of three, I got tired of the stories she would read me at naptime. I started telling her stories: Stories about my teddy bears and the little bathtub creatures I used to play with. The stories were adventures that they had when I wasn't around. The stories were filled with wars, treasure and terrifying caves and tunnels. I insisted that she write them down as I told them to her. Then she would mail them to an aunt in Seattle, who would type them up. They looked just like little books.

* * *

We lived on the edge of a swamp until I was nine. Past our house, the street narrowed and turned into a dirt road and a block and a half away was about a four-acre marsh that I always called The Great Swamp. My neighborhood friend and I used to explore there. One time we stole my older brother's BB pistol and hunted pinecones. We pretended the pinecones were Indians and shot them. Another time we came across a bird's nest. It was on the branch of a tree that had been loosened by a storm until it touched the ground. There were four tiny birds in it and one larger one. The larger one kept pecking at us when we tried to touch the smaller ones. Even though we were only six years old at the time, my friend and I didn't want to hurt the little birds, we only wanted to touch them. To feel their little feathers and the tiny heartbeats against our fingers. The big bird got very angry with us. So angry that we chased it away.

We picked the nest up to take it home. On the way to my house we met the teen-age son of another neighbor. He looked at the nest and we told him about the big bird and how we had chased it away with a stick. He told us that the big bird was the mother, and that since we had taken the nest, even if we put it back exactly where we had found it, she would never go back to it again and the baby birds would die. We were devastated. I stood holding the nest, looking at the baby birds and the teen-ager just shook his head at us, telling us without words how stupid we were.

I had an idea. I handed the nest to my friend and told him to go and put it back and wait and see if the mother would come back. I went home and wrote a note, printing in big block letters, telling the mother bird that we were sorry we had disturbed her nest, explaining that we didn't know what we were doing. Then I took the note and a safety pin and went back to the swamp. The mother bird hadn't come back. My friend was sitting on a log and crying. I showed him the note and then I pinned it to the nest. We both promised out loud to the invisible mother bird, wherever she might be, that we would never come back to bother her nest again. Then we went home.

We didn't go back to the swamp for three days. When we did, we snuck up quietly on the nest. The note was still pinned to the side. All the babies were dead.

At Easter, the year I was six, my brother gave me two baby chicks. The smaller of the two died within a week—I have always believed that the larger chick killed its box-mate; "trampled" to death was what I was told at the time, but how could such small creatures "trample" each other?—the one that survived, a rooster, I named Freddy, after a cousin, and raised as a pet. He would come to the call of his name and jump up on my shoulder and ride. I took him with me out playing, or exploring in the woods; I took him to the neighbors' houses. They were all amazed that a rooster could be a pet. A dog caught him once and shook him like a rag doll. The shaking broke some bones in his neck. He lived but his neck was crooked after that and his crow sounded like an old man's cough.

In August of that summer, my family was going away on a month's trip. I couldn't take the chicken with me. My father gave me a choice: Give Freddy to a farmer he knew out in the Valley; or sell him to the neighborhood butcher for a dollar. I don't think my father pressured me, and I don't know why, thinking back, that I remember the dollar figure before I even took Freddy to the butcher—I must have thought then, and still think, that it was a set-up pre-arranged deal; a dollar was a lot of money. I loved my father when I was six, but now . . . it was a rigged-deal, and I never had a choice. I sold Freddy to the butcher. He rode on my shoulder right up to the counter and, as I handed him over, he looked at me, his crooked neck twisted all around. I hid my eyes from him and scratched the silver dollar off the top of the counter.

Something's wrong here. I hadn't wanted to think or talk about Freddy. Now, I'm seeing his eye, his beak and his head on that bent neck. I have to stop this for a while.

*   *   *

What I was talking about was the way I would write things down as a way of solving problems. The letter to the mother bird obviously didn't work; neither did another letter I wrote when I was thirteen. From the time I was nine until I was fourteen my room was the lesser of two bedrooms on the main floor of a small house that my parents built. It was the first house my family owned. The room was small, just room for a bed, a dresser and a little worktable for me to use in doing homework. There was a picture of The Last Supper on the wall next to the bed, and a large glow-in-the-dark crucifix hanging on the wall at its foot. The room smelled faintly of rotten eggs from the sulfur paint on the crucifix and the last thing I would see at night was its glow from the wall.

When my parents went out one night in my thirteenth year, I sat in my father's chair in the living room and looked at a copy of a pocketbook-sized picture magazine called *Quick*—it was a mini version of *Life*.

I stared at a picture of Mitzi Gaynor. She was

wearing a tutu and her legs looked very long. I started to rub my penis. The more I looked at Mitzi Gaynor, the more I rubbed my penis. It got very hard and then, suddenly, I felt myself coming. I'd never touched myself before. I'd had a wet dream, once, in a motel room on a trip with my parents. It was a dream about a huge Negro maid. It scared me. I woke my mother up and told her that I thought I was sick. When I explained what had happened, she told me that I was all right; it was just that I was growing up. I didn't understand what she meant. I still thought that there was something wrong with me. But looking at the picture of Mitzi Gaynor and rubbing myself was so, so good, so natural that when I felt the spasms and saw the fluid come out of the end of my penis I was proud of myself. I had discovered a very wonderful, very private secret about myself. I had no idea of what it meant. It felt so good that I was sure that it was an end in itself.

I began to masturbate habitually, as often as I could. Then I found out what it was: It was "jacking off;" "beating off." And it was dangerous—a deadly habit that might make you go crazy or use up so much of the fluid that came out that you would never be able to do it again. Also the feeling I got from looking at Mitzi Gaynor (or the African women in *National Geographic*, or the models in art and photography magazines) had to do specifically with women, with girls and what you could do with them. I didn't know what that was. I got scared.

I wanted to quit, but, like any addict, I couldn't. So, I wrote a letter to Jesus. Looking at the smelly crucifix on my wall, I wrote Him a letter. "Dear Jesus," I wrote, "I promise never to masturbate again." I signed it. But then I didn't know what to do with it. I was frantic, but I wasn't crazy enough to believe that Jesus had a post office box. I didn't want anybody to find it, but I had to keep it—it was a signed document, a pact. So I hid it in the top drawer of my dresser. Things got worse for me; I couldn't stop jacking off, yet I had promised Christ that I would. I felt that I was both killing and damning myself.

Then, one day, when my mother was putting socks in that top drawer, she found the letter. "Did you write this?" she said. I nodded. "Do you *do* this?" she asked. I nodded again. She didn't say anything else, just walked out of my room, leaving me with my letter, The Last Supper, and the crucifix.

Two days later, without saying anything, she gave me a copy of a book, *The Facts of Life and Love for Teenagers*. I stayed in my room with the book.

"The penis becomes erect and is thrust into the vagina. A quick series of up and down motions ejaculates the semen." I can still quote that passage from memory. It was the most exciting, the most—romantic!—wonderful thing I had ever read. That was what it was all about! That's what I wanted from Mitzi Gaynor; I wanted the tutu off of her and to be inside of her moving up and down. I read the two sentences over and over and as I read them I masturbated joyfully. I knew the mysteries of the universe, and I held the answer in my own hand.

When I was fourteen, I moved out of that room and into a bigger bedroom in our finished basement. The glow-in-the-dark crucifix stayed upstairs; and I didn't go to Sunday school anymore.

Two years later I went to a whorehouse in Wallace, Idaho.

* * *

I need to talk to somebody. The goddamn loneliness is killing me. I need another therapy session. I drank too much vodka last night. And today I'm scared that it might be starting in again because I started drinking the minute I got up. I gagged on the first swallow and almost threw it up. If I let the cycle start again, I will be throwing up—that damn bitter, yellow bile; coughing and gagging until my stomach goes into convulsions. I don't want that to happen. I don't want this to get out of control.

So, I'll drink slowly through the day today and then try to go to sleep early. It's mental, I know. It's in my mind.

Last night it was raining heavily and then the temperature dropped and the rain turned to snow. I sat at the window of the cabin and watched the snowfall. Then I stoked the fire up and lay down on the rug in front of the fireplace and read. I read about the Donner Party. About their hopes and dreams and the trip West that turned them into madmen.

I had to stop reading and I put on my heavy coat and sat on the steps outside the cabin and watched the snowfall over the lake. Two big pines shielded me from the snow, but the wind off the lake was bitter cold.

I was holding the vodka bottle in my hands and drinking out of it, straight, so that I could feel the cheap vodka burn in my throat.

How did they do it? Not just the Donners. All of them. All the people who came west in the nineteenth century. The Donners were driven crazy by the land, or by their stupidity and their inability to deal with the land. But what about the Mountain Men who would kill buffalo or deer and then drink the warm blood and eat the innards raw? Or all the embittered young "Harvard Men," who took Greeley's advice; or the young Southern Gentlemen who went west to escape the dead post-Civil War South? How about those guys? What did they feel? Think? When they woke up in a cave in the mountains with snow falling all around them and only the hope of killing a rabbit to keep them alive? No voices. No other humans. Just the stray animal sounds of nature.

I shouted out across the lake; screaming into the dark, snow-filled air. Then I got up and walked down to the shore. I stood there and yelled, feeling the snow covering my face and hair. I didn't yell "Hello," or "Help," or any other sensible words. I just yelled sounds, mixed-up combinations of vowels and consonants.

Why did they do it? So many of them with so many different reasons, drawn to the West. What did they expect to find in the mountains and beyond? Did they want to be Indians or just take what the Indians had and make it like the East? They were all crazy!

I drained the vodka bottle and threw it out into the night. I heard it hit thin ice and bounce. Then it was quiet again, except for the sound of the wind in the trees and a howling sound that some kind of animal was making somewhere in the darkness.

The members of the Donner/Reed party ate each other's corpses when they began to starve; they talked about killing Indians for food. And history has judged them crazy—their trip a tragedy. But what about the rest of them? All the pioneers, the wanderers and the sojourners must have had very dark thoughts alone in the vastnesses at night in storms and with the terribly real fears they had of the strangeness all around them. And what they thought and felt they passed down. Those who survived the trip away from comfort and security told their children of the dangers and the dark thoughts—of murder, mutilation, cannibalism—passed through the generations until now, I'm sure, there isn't one of us who was born and raised out here where there are still mountains and storms and the silences of nature; not one of us who has heard a story about Indians, or about dark winters, who doesn't feel the land he was born to in his bones and in his nightmares doesn't see the inherited possibility to witness or commit the unspeakable.

There's not one of us who's not afraid.

*   *   *

When I went back to the cabin, I only slept for an hour or two, on the floor, with my clothes on, in front of the fire. The strange noises from the night almost drove me crazy.

Today there are about three inches of snow on the beach and the shoreline is frozen. You can see the snow line out on the lake: Five hundred yards is my guess, and then it's open water.

I can't stop it. I can't stop thinking.

David Denny, the youngest member of the Denny Party that crossed the continent from Illinois and became the first white settlers in what is now Seattle, spent the winter of his nineteenth year alone on Alki Point, jutting out into Puget Sound. He'd gone ahead of the rest of the party to scout out possible settlements. He sent a message back to them in

Portland and set about to build houses on the isolated point. He built part of a cabin, really just a lean-to, and then he cut his foot with an axe and was unable to work. The Indians stole his supplies and he spent the cold, wet winter alone in his lean-to, living off berries, nuts and clams he was able to dig from the beach; feverish and frightened.

I've always thought that the winter he spent alone on that beach, frightened, gimped-up, cold and hungry must have forged something good in his soul. I'm jealous of him; just like I'm jealous of my grandfather, and, in some strange way, of my father. All three of them were destroyed in the end by the world of men; by a growing, progressing world that they couldn't, or didn't want to, deal with. But the world that they did know, the world that they really lived in, inside of their hearts, was so much realer than any world that I have ever known. They lived in worlds of real things—it was different for each of them, and my rude father scoffed at the idealism of my rude grandfather, but in many ways it was the same world for all of them. A world where things and the words that men used to indicate them meant something; the language they shared without really ever knowing each other was a language of the senses—"Do you see that?" Can you smell that?" "Feel that?"

My father talking to the Chief of the Makah Tribe about insurance; my grandfather and his brother building cabins in the wilderness of the Rockies; and David Denny learning the language of the men who stole his food—what do we do now that is like any of that? Go and hide out at an abandoned cabin to drink, grieve and talk to ourselves?

If the wind, the voice of nature, frightened our

ancestors, we are frightened by clerks, by typed demands for money that we receive in the mail, by whoever makes and enforces our laws and by whatever it is that makes us break them. We are the damned, doomed Donner Party—all of us—wandering in a wilderness, ready to eat each other's flesh or be eaten ourselves. I really feel that way! Alone, frightened; more alone in the cities than I am out here at this winter, freezing lake.

I've got to stop this now. I'm writing all this down outside, looking up at the vastness of the water and ice in front of me, and I'm beginning to despair. And, my hands are numbing from the cold. I need to have another drink. Thank God for the vodka, if I weren't drinking all the time I would lie on the cabin floor and jack-off around the clock like some crazy chimpanzee.

* * *

"You see, I had to talk to you . . . to get some perspective . . ."

"Just like you have to drink."

"I don't have to drink. I choose to drink. It helps me to control things."

"What sort of things?"

"My emotions. My memories."

"Memories?"

"My past. The things I've done . . ."

I can feel myself about to cry. My hands are shaking and I've got a tremble in my shoulders. I've got to try to see him. Make him real. If I cry, I'll end up screaming.

"Yes. The . . . things . . . I've done . . ."

"Tell me what you mean."

"In my mind . . . some of it. But I killed my chicken, I killed the birds, my grandfather's banties. I would have killed the wino; my father, even my grandfather . . . "

"You didn't."

"I can taste the fucking blood in my mouth!"

My voice is echoing in the cabin. I hear "blood!" . . . "blood!" and his voice isn't there for me. It's up to me. He will be here if I can just control myself; just try to talk. Stop the pounding.

"Can you answer a question for me?"

"I'm not sure."

"Try? If . . . would it be . . . if I had been starving would I have eaten the dead Indian that Gary and I found in the alley?"

"Why do you ask me that?"

"Because I don't know! Would I have killed him?"

"You have to answer that."

"Jesus, Jesus! Don't do this to me. I don't know! Please, I don't even know if my life was ever real or not. You have to help me! I want to hurt someone . . . "

"Why? Why do you want to hurt another person?'

"Because none of it makes any sense. The world I should have known is dead and I am alone."

"You're pitying yourself."

"No! That's not it. I can't pity myself for not knowing something that I'm not sure ever even existed. I feel a tension in me that is a part of the world outside and yet I can't connect it and me. I'm lost. I'm home again. I'm even in the woods and I can't connect. I touch the ground, I hold the trees and I feel like I'm embracing dead bodies. My grandfather's brother, Hand-Axe Pete, who came west

with him to build the cabins in Glacier Park, wore women's underwear—lace panties. When my aunt Queenie told me that, I had some quick self-correcting reactions: First, he was a queer; second, he must have had some bad psychological problems; and, third, it's all right, there's nothing wrong with being a homosexual. Then I asked her why he did it and she replied: "I don't really know. I guess it was more comfortable. We never really thought about it." But me? I did have to think about it. I didn't have a choice. My goddamn mind went to work on Pete. You see, it's not the land that's dead, or the trees; it's me. Is it better to fuck a sheep or a cow? Pete was a lumberjack, a journeyman carpenter who liked to wear silk panties. Me? I've lost my bearings. He came west to what? Build? For the adventure? Just for the world? I went east to learn."

"What have you learned?"

"Nothing. Not a goddamned thing, except that I miss things and I don't even know what they are."

"What do you mean?'

"I mean . . . what I just said: A frontier carpenter in silk panties. My . . . what . . . Granduncle? I mean, when I was a kid and I walked into a restaurant and the door was a huge open mouth with great, thick red lips and enormous white teeth and I walked over the tongue and the restaurant was a giant coal-black head with a chef's hat on it, and I went there after the age of six, after my mother had told me that Negroes might easily kill me. I know what I think now, what I can create for my feelings then, but was I afraid that the mouth would shut and, like Jonah, I would be trapped with all my relatives in the stomach of a titanic angry black man? I know that I didn't think that the Coon Chicken Inn was grotesque or hideously racist and laugh at it with heavy irony. That's me now. Then? It was an amusement park, turned frightening by my mother's revelations of social realities that I could only understand in nightmare terms. How much fun it was—Pinocchio on Pleasure Island— until my mother made me aware that all the happy Negroes waiting the tables were human beings. And they were my enemies . . . and I'm sure that I knew that they were my enemies because I knew their secret: that they were niggers. And they would kill me if they knew that

I could say the word, and I was too young, too little to kill them first. So, I walked into the mouth, like a spy, in secret, thrilling terror. I was a white scout sneaking into an Indian camp and watching their wild night, firelight dancing—fascinated and terrified by the painted faces.

That was it. The fantasy. Me, heroic, risking death, Errol Flynn as Custer fighting Anthony Quinn as Crazy Horse; kill or be killed, unless we counted coup on each other and stood tall as men in the wilderness. Blood brothers bonded in the fear and love of nature. Me. The scout, the spy, the frontiersman, the mountain man—the man who could talk to the Indians, who knew the coyotes and the panthers. The Westerner.

From the time that I was fourteen, my parents went to California every winter for four months and every summer for at least a month, leaving me on my own in Spokane. My friend Gary would stay with me part of the time. We'd charge food at the grocery store and live like two teen-age grown-ups; taking care of the house, being responsible. Late at night we would listen to '45s and talk about what we would do if the Russians invaded. We figured that Seattle would be blown up by an atomic bomb and that we would see the burst of the explosion over the mountains and across the desert 300 miles away in Spokane. They wouldn't bomb us, because they would want all the farmland. We figured that everybody in Spokane would panic except for us and our close friends. We would get arms and food and go up into the hills south of town, with Manito Golf Course as a focus point, and from there fight a guerrilla war out of the old farmhouses that dotted the landscape of the Palouse. And we would marry our high-school girlfriends and begin to raise families on the New Frontier of America. See, we knew that the United States would be gone as a country, but we could start again.

"Why would you marry if you were fighting a guerrilla war?"

"Oh, that was a major part of it. You see, we—at least I—wanted very badly to fuck Doris Day (particularly if she was Calamity Jane and I was Howard Keel playing opposite her), but, along with and, maybe, even more than fucking her we (I) wanted to marry her. My mother would have been horrified if I told her that I fucked Doris Day, but she would have been deliriously happy if I married her. All our girlfriends were Doris

Day in our fantasies. The fucking and the Mom and Dad pictures all came together in our heads. We didn't think of ourselves as just fighters—it wasn't a grubby war where we could die. We were a mixed breed, taking the best of the Indians and the old, original white settlers. We could kill the enemy and build the churches at the same time. We would be settling a New America.

Fathers and Mothers of the land. It never occurred to us that we could lose in our sorties against the Russian invaders, or that war was sophisticated, modern and deadly. We had seen the WW II war pictures, but we preferred the images we held of things like *Drums Along the Mohawk*: Henry Fonda running in the woods chased by savages, yet making it home, safe, into the arms of Claudette Colbert.

"This isn't 'bloody.' You were talking about blood and violence. This is romance."

"*This* is a goddamn fantasy! You want an example of what we did in reality? There was a residential area about two miles north of my family's house in Spokane. It was really fancy; rich Catholics lived there. There was a street that was a steep hill that ran into a little park, the street split at the park and went both ways around it. Gary and I drove down from my house, parked on a side street and then, playing spy, being covert, snuck into the Indian Camp of the Rich Catholics. The Catholics parked their cars on the street and they never locked them because Spokane was a safe town, particularly in their neighborhood. I snuck up to a car about halfway down the steep hill. It had a clear shot at the park. I opened the door and released the emergency brake and took it out of gear. Gary did the same thing to a car parked five feet behind mine. Then I crossed the street and let a car on the other side loose. We raced for the bushes as the cars rolled, accelerating, towards the park. One, two, three, they all jumped the sidewalk and with great crashes hit each other and the trees. There was a wonderful explosion and then the cars and the park burst into flame and the Rich Catholics flicked on their porch lights and came out on their lawns to watch. Gary and I snuck back to my car, exultant in the knowledge that we had let their horses loose. Our night raid was a success."

"What do you mean 'let their horses loose'?"

"You've seen Westerns haven't you? You let the Indians' horses loose so they can't chase you."

Silence.

"And. We waited two weeks and went back again. We got five cars that time. And got on the front page of the *Review*."

"Mischief. Malicious mischief."

"Any kid could have done it, right? Rebel against authority? When I've told people about it before, I tried to make it sound political. Fashionable. Masses against classes stuff, so that I could make myself out a teen-age radical. That's all bullshit. We did it for the fun. Playing White Scout. And Indian. We were White Indians, taking a shot at the Settlers. We were outlaws. Nice middle-class kids by day, we were bandits and raiders by night. There was a lot of fantasy in the things we did. But, everything was very real too. We wanted something."

"Were you jealous of the people you call the Rich Catholics?"

"You mean did we want those cars we smashed? No, that wasn't it at all. Another time, four of us snuck in at night into a real mansion, up on Cliff Drive with a view over the whole town and the Valley. We knew the kid in the family and knew that they were out of town and we knew how to get in. We trashed the whole house. We smashed dozens of their wine glasses and all the china, tossing the glasses into the fireplaces. We knocked over and broke their statues, and scratched their paintings and broke them over our knees. We pissed on the beds. A guy named Stan took a shit on their big banquet table. We stayed all night and littered the place with beer bottles and cigarette butts. We didn't do that because we were jealous of them. We didn't steal anything. We did it . . . "

"Why?"

"God damn it, I couldn't have told you then. I'm not sure I can get it straight now. Except that I know I'd do all those things again. It was like we were fighting for something and we didn't really know what it was."

Silence.

*   *   *

I need to think some things out by myself now. I need more to drink. Maybe I need to go outside into the woods. I've got to let two or three things unscramble in my head before I talk again. Anyway, the questions aren't getting me anywhere.

God, it's so beautiful in the woods. It's bitter cold but the sun is brilliant. The trees are filled with snow and there's no wind to blow it down. There must be half a foot on the ground as I come to the top of the ridge. No cattle anywhere, they're probably down by the outbuildings in the valley, eating. Brushing the snow off a branch I can press my face into the pine needles.

My problem is that I want to think that everybody is as smart as I am; when I discover that they're not, then I don't want to be around them. That means I don't want to be around anybody.

I've got to follow one thing at a time. Chase one strand down, and then go on from there. For instance: Fucking Doris Day. Now, jacking-off over a picture of Mitzi Gaynor is one thing—Mitzi was showing flesh; a tease in her tutu, it didn't take much imagination to see and feel the gorgeous sweet cunt under that tiny skirt—but Doris Day was something entirely different. The point of wanting to fuck Doris Day was that it was impossible. Doris Day was no coquette, what she offered was the ultimate in clean, good girl wholesomeness. She was marriage. And marriage like our mothers represented it to us; marriage without sex. Sure, if you married Doris Day you could fuck her, but probably what would happen would be that the anticipation would be so incredible that you would die of some sort of ecstasy the second you got inside her. It would be like that spider that kills its mates. Sandy and Ann and Topper were Doris Day to me in high school—oh God! I wanted so desperately to fuck them, but they wouldn't. I could touch them, but marriage, marriage, marriage. So, from the age of sixteen I went to whorehouses. In Wallace, Kellogg, Iron City, Priest River, Aberdeen, and, last and best, Walla Walla. My friends and I, and the miners, loggers and migrant farm workers. Five dollars straight; ten dollars for a half and half. One of my friends used to get in the trunk of the car and jack-off during the forty-five minute drive through Fourth of July Canyon from Coeur d'Alene to Wallace, so that he could last longer and get more for his five dollars. Poor Dale, when we introduced ourselves to a group of whores one afternoon in Priest River, a girl named Marge said: "Dale! I know your father, George." We used to see faculty members from our college coming down the backstairs of the Ritz and the Ashford in Walla Walla. We'd be sitting in our cars drinking beer and catcall at them and then duck down. My dearest friend, Frank, used to go with us in Walla Walla, but never bought. One night I pressured him, paid his five dollars myself, and he went into a room with one of the girls. He came out crying fifteen minutes later. "She looked like my mother," he said.

From sixteen to twenty-two, I was a virgin in the straight world. I loved my girlfriends. I went steady and got pinned in college. But, even though I loved them and they said they loved me, we never had intercourse. It was Doris Day. It's not that I wanted to fuck movie stars, I wanted, so badly, to fuck my girlfriends, but it was always marriage. I felt like Henry Fonda as Wyatt Earp in *My Darling Clementine*. I knew that he wanted to fuck Clementine even though she was supposedly Doc Holliday's intended, but he was honorable and chaste about it. She was pure. A real Western Ideal. The girl you must, if you were, yourself, a Westerner, protect and honor. Her virtue was the last bastion of civilization. My problem was that I was more Holliday than Earp. My heart was split and I grew to love the whores I knew and mated my spirit to them. My father was better off getting drunk with loggers or Indians than he was in a corporate boardroom; I was happier in a whorehouse than I was in a middle-class living room.

And that's why I sent Rich Catholics' cars crashing into the park.

I couldn't fuck Doris Day, but I could spray my jism all over a picture of Mitzi Gaynor, or I could wrap myself in a whore's arms and have her call me "honey," and praise the size and strength of my cock. I always chose the last. I was just another Mountain Man, wrapped in furs and drunk as a god. When I was fifteen, my friend John told me that his girlfriend had given him a chair-job when he was in the seventh grade. He didn't tell me what it was. When I was twenty, I asked Janet, in the Ashford in Walla Walla, for a chair-job. She didn't ask me what it was; she did it. Then I knew.

In Walla Walla, whorehouses were legal. The girls had to go to a doctor every week to be checked out for any diseases. One day, I was waiting to see a doctor, and Vicki from the Ritz walked in. She checked with the nurse and then came over to talk to me. It was pretty obvious that we knew each other. The nurse was the wife of the Dean of the college. It was a small college, so she knew me too. The next week I was called into the Dean's Office. He lectured me, and, in return, I smart-assed him. "I know, Dean, but for me the spirit may be willing, but the flesh is very weak." I didn't tell him that Vicki was one of my best friends and that lots of times I would just go down to the Ritz and hang out with her in the kitchen and drink beer. He wanted me to be a role model; after all, I was president of my fraternity.

It's all fucked-up, isn't it?

Or, maybe it's not.

I knew of guys—and even met a couple of them at the Green Lantern in Walla Walla—who would beat up the whores or trash the whorehouse. They'd go to jail, and three of them got thrown out of school for fighting a bunch of Mexican migrants out back of the Ashford. My friends and I—particularly me, since I would go alone a lot—were always perfect gentlemen. We might be drunk, but we were there—again, particularly me—for love.

The summer I was seventeen, John and Gary and I started going to the State Line between Coeur d'Alene and Spokane on Saturday nights. We did it because we got served without id there and also to fight. The bars at the Line were big shit-kicking live band country music joints and they would be loaded on Saturday with farm-boys, pea-picking migrants, bikers and white trash from all over Northern Idaho and Northeastern Washington. We were all there to get drunk and fight. We were town kids and loved the idea of bouncing some rube's head off a car in the parking lot. Gary would always pick the fight. He was the smallest and had the worst mouth. Then John or I would do the actual fighting. Everybody was so drunk that the fights were usually just a lot of wild punches and once in a while a kick in the balls, so nobody ever really got hurt. No weapons. Just anger and energy; cowboy stuff.

Or, as I used to say, "counting coup" like the Indians.

When I was eighteen, we went down the Pendleton Roundup in Oregon, which was then the biggest rodeo in the West. We told our parents that we were going to the rodeo, but what we intended was a good road drunk and we figured we might be able to fuck some Indians, since a whole bunch of tribes held a pow-wow along with the rodeo. It was night when we got to Pendleton; the rodeo was in full swing, but we wanted the Indian camps. The Indians weren't staying in motels; they were doing the tourist/Indian village thing, with the tee-pees, the campfires and the native garb and paint. In the daytime. A few of them played cowboy and Indian in the rodeo shows, but at night most all changed out of the costumes into jeans and shirts and got drunk in the camp. The women would cook up fry-bread and stuff, and the men would just stand around and drink and fart and laugh.

We were pretty drunk ourselves by the time we drove into the camp. We'd gotten our adrenaline up by talking about how three guys from Lewis and Clark High School were finally going to fuck Sacajawea. We were willing to pay her twenty-five bucks for a three-way, or, if we could get her into the car and out of the camp, we figured that it would be free. We pulled our car past the first ring of tee-pees, and Gary rolled his window down and yelled at the first Indian he saw, a guy who had been standing, drinking with a bunch of his buddies but turned to look at us. "Hey, Buck," Gary called. The guy started to walk towards us. "Where can we get some 'skin poon-tang?" A beer bottle crashed against the side of the car, and the Indian was running towards us. And not just him, the whole gang of buddies—maybe ten of them (although we always said that it been at least thirty)—yelling and running. "Fucking, drunk scum-bag Warhoops!" Gary yelled and rolled up his window. We locked the doors. And then they were all over the car. We were yelling, "Fuck you!" and giving them the finger, and they were pounding on the car, breaking beer bottles and, then, rocking the car. "These fucking 'skins are trying to kill us," John said. I started popping the car from first to reverse, trying to shake them off. All the time we were yelling at each other. Finally, I dug out in reverse and knocked one guy off into a clump of brush. His buddies ran to attend to him. We got away. We bought a case of malt liquor and drove the three hours to Walla Walla and the Ritz.

So, we escaped a massacre. Most of the time with Indians, it was just catching one or two of them drunk in a white tavern and ridiculing them. Name-calling. Sometimes we'd carry "funny-money," fake bills and give them to panhandling Indians outside the State Liquor Store and then wait and laugh at them when they went in and tried to buy wine and were thrown out. No fights. I never hit an Indian. It was almost the same thing with Mexicans when I was in college. Walla Walla was flooded with illegal, wetback laborers for the wheat and pea harvests in the summer. They were carted around in big open bed trucks, jammed in like sardines, sweating and laughing. One hot afternoon we got caught by the cops because we were passing the wetback trucks on the highway and tossing bottles of beer into the swarm of people. Two guys got knocked off the truck in a scuffle for the beer at thirty miles an hour. The driver got our license number and the state cops picked us up. We told them that we thought we were just tossing empties and didn't mean to throw anything into the truck. A lame excuse, but the cops hated the Mexicans and they were happy with any excuse to forget about the incident. We never found out if the laborers who fell off the truck were hurt, or killed, or whatever happened to them. We didn't like the Mexes going in the whorehouses and neither did the girls. We were sure they all had clap. They were greasier and dirtier than the off-res Indians. They were drunk too, but in a different way. The Mexes laughed and shouted when they were drunk, the Indians just staggered around, like they were asleep on their feet and fell down on the sidewalk a lot. Pioneer Square in Seattle was like a human mosaic, with passed out Indians spread all over the paved park. Indians never went into the whorehouses. They weren't allowed; just like they weren't allowed in most white taverns.

Indians worked as whores, though. My friend, Warren, was so excited in finding an Indian woman in a house in Aberdeen that he beat on the door of the room I was in and yelled, over and over: "I got an Indian! I got an Indian!"

Nobody wanted to fuck a Mexican. We thought of them the same way my grandfather thought of Chinese; unwanted, scummy creatures. We only had one Indian at Lewis and Clark High School, a big, stolid girl named Ida. She was President of Girl's Fed. She was a Christian Indian and talked very slowly and carefully as though she were speaking a foreign language. She smiled all the time. Nobody wanted to fuck Ida, either.

We didn't see many Indian girls in the towns. We had a fantasy that they looked like Debra Paget in *Broken Arrow*, but when I went to the reservations with my parents when I was little—my mother and I went with my father sometimes when he did insurance business with the tribes; he would meet with the men and my mother would shop for Indian baskets—the girls I saw looked unhealthy and dirty. Still, all of us wanted to have sex with an Indian woman. That was the most exotic thing we could imagine—it would be like fucking the land itself. I would still like to fuck an Indian. Deep, dark eyes; high, sharp cheekbones; jet-black, thick hair.

* * *

If I'm not snowed-in here—and I might be—if I could get my car out, I could drive to Coeur d'Alene town and then out the Interstate through Fourth of July Canyon, an hour tops to Wallace. Would they have any Indian whores in Wallace, or Kellogg, or

Iron City? Are there still whorehouses there? I can't risk it. I'm too drunk to drive. And if I got into the car, I could get stuck and freeze to death in the snow; or if I made it out of here to the highway, I could have an accident; or if I got there, Wallace could have been cleaned-up and sanitized just like Spokane was, and there'd be family restaurants and ice-cream parlors instead of the miners' bars and whorehouses. I've seen too much death, of towns as well as people. I don't need any more. I'm safer here, in my mind. In my past.

* * *

When I went east, my cousin Maynard took me to dinner at the Harvard Club in New York. He and I were the only people in our gigantic family of aunts, uncles and cousins to ever go to college. He was afraid that education would hurt me in that it would turn me against my rude, uneducated family. He was wrong. It didn't fracture me. I learned easily that I couldn't talk about the world I had lived in, because to me it was real and to the strangers I met—and married—it was some sort of aberration. I didn't reform in the East; I just developed more and more of a veneer that I hated, an affectation of civilization. I could tell stories of what I had done and what I had seen, but they were moral tales always including a coda of: "I did that then, not now." What was always left out was: "But, I would do it again, except that this time I would follow it all the way into the wilderness."

I would wear silk panties in the woods, if they felt good.

That's easy to say, glib, facile. I might wish for the courage to wear silk panties; I might wish for the courage to have the desire to wear silk panties—without thinking about it, without making a conscious decision, without making it some sort of political move; without it being something that others had to know about. Just doing it. A creature of instinct. That's what I've lost—or, maybe never really had—my instincts. I think that I was born kin to the Indians. Kin to the animals. I think my grandfather was, David Denny was, and, even my father was; and that I might have been. I'm not blaming my mother, but she surely "schoolmarm'd" me. She didn't want another anachronistic Mountain Man in her family, not like her father or the man she married; she wanted a model Village Citizen, the minister, the mayor, the schoolteacher, even the successful dry-goods merchant.

* * *

See, I know that Crazy Horse shape-changed. I know that he's still alive. And I've known that for a long time. That's a secret that I can't ever tell anyone because if I do, I'll break the bond.

He is waiting for me to find him. Somewhere in the woods, sometime, I will smell something that isn't pine or fir or squirrel or deer and it will be his soul. When I was five years old and lost in the Great Swamp I smelled him and he led me out; and, when I was lying, tied to a Canadian bed, dying of liver failure, I know I smelled his soul and he brought me back. He's here now. He moves throughout the West. Now, he's here, by the lake. I have to purify myself before I can find him. That's why I have to think. I'm not Keseberg, and Keseberg is not waiting in the woods for me. It's Crazy Horse. The blood I taste is my blood, it's his blood.

I am not my mother's son.

*   *   *

The snow is coming down heavily now. There must be a storm in the Coeur d'Alenes and the Kootenais. It's too dark to go too far into the woods, but I can taste the air by walking along the lakeshore and working my way up the small rock faces of the hills. There's no ice on the rocks, so my gloves and boots grip well. Now I'm sitting on top of Pilot Rock, itself, facing straight out into the lake. There are coves off to either side of me. To my right, I see the light from the fire in my cabin reflecting off the lake; to my left is the darkness of the beach and the woods. No moon. If I could see across the lake I would see the logs at the mouth of the St. Joe. The air is so clean and pure. I can eat the snow. I'm drinking the vodka straight out of the bottle I carried up here in my coat. It burns my throat, but I gulp snow and I feel giddy and cool and warm inside. I wish, right now, that I could fly. I'd like to stand up on the very tip of Pilot Rock and soar into the black sky over the lake. The wind would carry me, soaring like an eagle, into the mountains to some other place, some other lake, where no white man had ever been before; maybe even no man, and I could find it all there, in the pure pines, the mountain ferns and grasses, all those secrets that we have hidden ourselves from. And I wouldn't be afraid, because I wouldn't think to be afraid. I would be there and I would be a part of the world. And I would touch hands with Crazy Horse and between us we would raise my father from his grave.

And I sit here in the night, staring into the dark and listening. I know that I am surrounded by life.

The tree I am leaning my back against is alive; I can hear the small, night sounds of animals and, under the lake's ice, fish are alive and feeding. There is music here, but I have to drink and talk to myself. I chatter away in my head, trying to make everything fit into sentences; moving back and forth in my past, remembering in fits and starts what I did and what was done around me. I imagine the loneliness. And I grieve for a life that I lived and that I didn't live. I want to fly out of my body. I want to fly out of the world and, yet, most of all, I want to have the snow melt for an instant and be able to bury my face in the fresh fragrant earth.

I'll climb down from the rock and go back to the cabin. I'll fix the fire and lie down in front of it and drink some vodka and read and see if I can sleep and I will try to think again tomorrow. I hurt now. I have gone too far, but I can't turn back. I must follow the road I feel with the bareness of my heart.

* * *

Why did I want to kill the wino we picked up in Pioneer Square? I was the one who suggested it. Warren, Pat, a friend of Warren's named Bill and I had been drinking all day. At night we went down to First Avenue and went to the peep shows. We were just banging around. Pat told the manager of one of the arcades that Warren was jacking-off in a peep-booth and the guy threw Warren out. That kind of stuff. We dropkicked a basketball we'd been playing with over the viaduct. We were being bad-boys. Then we went into a bar and a wino tried to hit us up for money. I told him that we would give him ten bucks if he would get us some pussy. He said, "Sure . . . sure," and Warren went and got his car and we got in it with the bum. No reason for it. He didn't know what he was doing, had no idea what was happening. We just pushed him in

the car. In the front seat, next to Warren. Pat and Bill and I sat in the back. I whispered to Pat, "Let's kill this fuck." "Yeah," Pat giggled, "he smells so bad he deserves to die. He's a bad loser." I leaned forward and said to the wino: "Forget about the pussy. We know you're worthless. You couldn't find pussy if your life depended on it. So, we're just going to finish you off, put you out of your misery." He stared at me and tried to laugh, but Bill put his hands on his shoulders and said: "It's for real, fucker. You're dying." And the guy started to cry and scream and we drove off into the night. We were laughing and Bill kept hitting the bum on the back of the head and the bum kept screaming, a high, hysterical sob.

Bill grabbed the wino by the hair and said: "Shut up, you fuck! We'll let you live if you suck us off. And," he shoved the bum's head down and across the front seat, "you start with Warren!"

Warren hit the bum on the side of the head and knocked him against the car door. "You had your chance, pal," Bill said; "If Warren doesn't want you, you got no reason to live. He'd let a chipmunk give him a blow-job."

In the laughter and the screaming inside the car, I could feel that it was real. We were actually ready to kill the wino. All of us. "Go to the Arboretum," I said to Warren, "nobody's going to be there." "A good place to dump the body," Pat said. The wino stopped screaming and we stopped laughing. He was just crying and sweating and drooling. He smelled like a fucking skunk.

We drove across the city and into the Arboretum in silence. Warren pulled off the road onto a drive beside the Japanese Gardens. It was pitch black outside.

I got out of the car and walked around it to the front passenger door. I opened it and the bum looked up at me. He looked like an animal; blank-eyes, mouth open, gasping. I pulled him up by the front of his shirt. He was a dead weight. I dragged him away from the car into the dark. Nobody else got out and nobody said anything. I dragged him to the top of a little hill leading down into the sculptured Japanese Garden. I held him up and said to him: "Live in Beauty." Then I pushed him off into the night and down the hill. I couldn't see him but I heard him crawl and then, groaning, stagger to his feet.

I went back to the car and got in the front seat where the wino had been sitting. He had pissed his pants and the seat was soaked, so I got in the back seat again. "You're a good Christian boy," Pat said.

* * *

You reach a certain point and then you do or you don't. And what's the difference if it's dark and there's no moon and you can feel the mountains and the water all around you; or, if you're at a still, flat point on the high desert, in the pitch-night, listening to the creatures cry? At those times it's easy to feel like Kit Carson and you want to find Crazy Horse because you want to be the one, even if you're the only one who knows it, to drive the stake into the world's heart. Or you want to crawl away in the night to a secret cave and scream at the walls.

When it's really dark night in the West, you're never in a city or a town; even on the most brightly lit main street, you can feel the earth and even smell it and you want to close your eyes and never see the buildings or feel the concrete again. I remember this feeling as a little kid. It frightened me then, because it made me so alone, but, even with the fear, there was an excitement that thrilled me, a power, a connection that I never felt in my ordinary life. When I first heard of the Indians I imagined that my feelings were what theirs must have been. I would dream-vision the woods and the high grasses around

Spokane filled with Indians, and, later, when I wandered the streets of the Indian bars at night with my teen-age friends—or alone—my imagination fought to pull them away from the squalor and despair and tear the buildings down and smell their horses and campfires.

Or, I wanted to hurt them.

*   *   *

Something is going on now. I am focusing clearly on the present—it's probably just for the moment—but it is happening. I am almost snowed in here. My brother told me a story about the farmer who first owned the property behind the beach. He would get snowed in regularly. The road in to the lake winds through the high hills above the meadows and is dirt and one lane and is never plowed. So one winter he decided he had to get out. He had a car and he set out to drive across and down the lake, which he assumed was completely frozen. He got about a half mile from shore and the car sank—the middle of the lake was thin ice and mush—he escaped, but the lake is so deep that they never found the car again. Could I get out now, even with snow tires and chains? I doubt it. A Ford Falcon is hardly an all-weather vehicle. What then? I know what certain members of the Donner Party did, but I'm alone. What would Jedediah Smith or Jim Clyman do? What did they do when they surely were snowed in in the Sierras or Rockies? They had no cars; maybe not even horses. Alone, on foot, what does one do when nature surrounds him? Thinking rationally, I know that this is just cheap melodrama. If I wanted to kill myself, why didn't I just rent a room in a Spokane transient hotel, buy a gun and do the job? Why bother to come out here and get drunk and moon over Crazy Horse?

Why did I want to talk to myself so badly that I came out to this frozen lake?

Well, this shit gets me nowhere.

I need to drink a little more and summon up a vision of my father.

My father had been forced by his immigrant father to work eight hours a day and twelve a day on weekends cleaning the Seattle Public Market and turn over all his wages to him in order to go to high school. He was the only one of his family to get a high school diploma. Maybe as a consequence of this, he hated people who had gone to college. He also hated people who made less money than him. He was in awe of those who, starting at the bottom as he did, made a lot of money; millionaires who, as did he, said "ain't" and "them guys" all the time. He toadied to the professional class and loathed the landed rich; "the coupon-clippers." He hated Jews; feared and despised Blacks; and sold insurance to Indians (he was even made an honorary member of several tribes, primarily due to the quality of the bourbon he brought to his meetings with the sachems). He disdained homosexuals. He was a womanizer. He was a drunk.

Before I bottomed out on booze the last time, I spent at least the last three months having long conversations with my father. As I lay alone in the bed in my rented room just coming into consciousness, having collapsed into bed after a day and night's drinking and rested and half-slept for a few hours, he would manifest in a chair across from me. We would talk, about his life, mine and the world we lived in, and then he would get malicious; his teeth and nails would begin to grow, he would snarl; and I, like Huck Finn's Pap, would be sure that the Angel of Death in the form of my father had come to seize me. I would stop the hallucination with a gulp from the bottle I kept beside my bed. I could then throw up the yellow bile and begin the day, safe from the further madness of delirium.

God, how I feared him. How I hated him. How I loved him. As a young boy my mother raised me and I never knew him. She told me that I wasn't like him, and that one night, unique among many filled with terror, when he came home drunk and I had been deputized, at age nine, to get up and wait while my mother and brother searched the bars for him; when I sat in his chair saying the Lord's Prayer over and over to myself, and he came in and I went to help him and he, not recognizing me, knocked me down the dark basement stairs; that night, above all others, I believed my mother was right. I was not him.

That night I cried at the bottom of the stairs, afraid to go up. I heard him fall down in the bedroom. I stayed in the dark until my mother came home and found me. After that I saw him drunk many times. He embarrassed me. He humiliated me. But he never touched me again. From the time I was fourteen and my parents went to Palm Springs for the winter for the first time and left me in Spokane, I never needed him again. I never needed either one of them again. Still and all, like a young gun-punk in an old Western town wanted a showdown with the famous gunslinger, I wanted to beat him at his own game; out-drink him. I did.

Fuck him.

* * *

You want to know something?

If you want to tell me.

This is like talking to myself.

It is, isn't it? Go ahead.

I was fifteen. Just turned fifteen. I wanted to go to the Spot for Friday night dances, but I was afraid to. I didn't know how to dance and I was afraid of the older kids. But they also had mixers going on at the old Eagles Hall in Spokane, and they weren't just for kids. Anybody could go. Lots of lonely older guys and women who worked as waitresses or barmaids would be there on Saturday nights. They never checked ID at the door, and I knew that none of the kids I wanted to be like would be there. One night my friend and neighbor, Bob, and I decided to go. We got there at nine and it was already really crowded. I felt like a little kid. There was a lot of smoking and drinking all around us, even on the dance floor. The Spot was just for teenagers, so there was no drinking allowed, but the Eagles encouraged drinking. They had three bars in the Hall. It was strictly country music, and it seemed like at least half the people in the place were singing along with the records. Dancing, yelling, singing and drinking. Couples were groping each other up against the walls or out on the dance floor.

Bob and I went to one of the bars and got beers with no questions asked about age. Then we stood up against a wall and looked around. We'd gone to the Eagles to try to drink and get some sex. We didn't know how to dance; we didn't know how to drink; and neither one of us had ever had any sexual experience, except for jacking off. We just wanted, that's all; just wanted.

The women who were dancing and hanging

around didn't look at all like the girls we went to school with. A lot of them had big breasts and really heavy lipstick. They were older and we knew that they'd give us sex if we could get close enough to them. We figured they were sluts; girls who worked at the movie theaters or drive-ins, or, maybe farm girls from south of town or out in the Valley. We stood and watched them, drinking beer and mumbling to each other about their breasts; about how they bounced when they danced and how some of them, who were just wearing T-shirts and no bras, were showing nipples. We both got hard-ons and didn't know what to do about it. Bob said that he was afraid that he was going to come in his pants. My head was spinning. So I said to Bob: "Let's go in the men's room and get a couple of stalls and jack-off. Then we'll feel better." He agreed.

The men's room was way at the back of the Hall. We didn't see anybody else when we walked in, but as we were walking past the urinals a guy came out of the first stall. He was older, probably in his twenties or thirties, and real wild looking; shaggy hair, stubble beard and eyes that jumped all over the place. He was short and skinny, pale-faced and wearing filthy jeans and an old flannel shirt.

"I got something for you guys," he said, moving out in front of us. "Some eight-pagers. You guys got any eight-pagers?" He held out what looked like a bunch of comic strips from the newspaper stapled together. "I got Popeye. Maggie and Jiggs." He opened one of the little books and showed us a page. It was a picture of Popeye with an enormous hard-on and Olive Oyl taking the head of it in her mouth.

"You want these?" Of course we did, they were

really dirty, just from looking at one picture we knew that.

Bob and I looked at each other. "What do you want for them?" I said.

"No money," he said, "just a favor."

"What favor?" I said.

"I want you," he pointed at me, "to come into this stall with me for just a minute. I want to show you something."

"Show me here."

"I don't have much time," his eyes were tearing, "you want these books, you step in there with me. I'm not gonna hurt you. I just want to show you something. Something you never seen."

What the hell. I was scared, but I wanted the books and I knew Bob was there and we were in the Eagles and so nothing really awful could happen. He wasn't going to kill me.

"Give my friend the books."

"I'll give him one. You get the other after you look."

He gave Bob the Maggie and Jiggs, and I followed him into the stall. He went in backwards and, standing up, straddled the toilet bowl. I was facing him with my back to the open door of the stall. He undid his pants with a swipe of his hand and it fell out. I never had seen anything like it before. It was a real horse-cock. I'd heard about them—cocks a foot long—but never believed that the stories were true.

He grinned at me and stroked it. "You like it?" he said. He got hard in just an instant. I was dizzy. It was so big that I thought I was dreaming. "You want to touch it?" His voice was soft, almost gentle. "Go ahead. I know you want to. I want you to." I did want to.

And I did. I touched the head. It was rough, like some kind of animal hide. I put my hand around it and my fingers barely touched. Then he shot on me. Without any warning, he spasmed and spasmed and came all over my hand, on the front of my pants' legs, on my shoes. I backed up, out of the stall. He was laughing and grinning at me. He reached into his shirt pocket and took out a handful of the eight-pagers and threw them at me. I ran for the door and out across the Hall dance-floor and out the front door. There was snow piled on the edge of the sidewalk on Howard Street, I plunged my hands into it and then threw my whole body down on it.

I never went back to the Eagles again. When I left, Bob grabbed the eight-pagers up off the men's room floor and ran out after me, leaving the guy talking to himself in the stall.

The eight-pagers were just as dirty as we thought they'd be. Mostly blow job stuff—Olive and Popeye, Maggie sucking Jiggs; but there was, in a third book, a whole four-page segment of Li'l Abner fucking Daisy May. When I looked at them I felt like Wimpy. All he did was jack-off like some chimp and eat hamburgers.

What do you think of that story?

What do you think of it?

Jesus! It happened. I did it. I wanted to feel some woman's tits, and I ended up helping some creep jack-off. Live in Beauty, huh? No, No, No. I'm not feeling sorry for myself . . . I just don't know why these are the kind of things that live in my mind. Dead Indians, bums, creeps, my father drunk at the Elk's Club pushing me out the door when I was trying to get a cab to take us home—Christ, I was fourteen . . . no, thirteen, then, and I see the picture clear as a new morning. All of this stuff. I remember after I ate out a whore in an Iron City whorehouse, when I came back out to the car I got into a fight—a real knock-down, roll on the ground fist-fight—with my friend Doug, because he said I was a queer for eating her, and said that he hoped that I got syph. Do you see what I mean?

Of course.

No, really, do you? I mean, the whore was so pretty. She smelled like flowers, like those wild mountain flowers that grow in the Coeur d'Alenes and the Kootenais, and she had me in her mouth and I was as hard as I could have ever imagined being and I was just eighteen; and she looked up at me and smiled and said: "Would you like to put your mouth on me?" I'd done that with my girlfriend Sandy, but this was different. This was a woman with a beautiful, thick black bush of hair, and she had just taken my cock out of her beautiful mouth to ask me. There was nothing in the world that I wanted to do more than put my mouth on her, my tongue in her. I loved her so much. You know, I can see her now, naked, in this room, and she just floods it. Her smell, her taste, the way her eyes looked at me; her smile, the way she moved her tongue on my cock. What it felt like to be inside her! Looking at her beautiful face.

God!

What?

Why did Doug and I have to fight out in back of an Iron City whorehouse over her? Why couldn't we just let it alone? Why didn't Bob and I beat up that freak in the Eagles? We were just kids, but we could've done it. Why did I have to get his come all over me and then end up fighting one of my best friends because I fell in love with a beautiful woman? I guess I wanted it all, or else none of it would have happened. I guess I could have married her, too. In my mind, I had, at least for that night, in Iron City. Now, I can't even remember her name. I don't know if I ever knew it. I must have, for a few seconds, known some name, whatever whore's name she called herself. I can still taste her cunt; see her eyes; feel the texture of her hair. But she's just beautiful in my mind, the wild-flower smell mixed with the antiseptic smell of a dimly lit room on the second floor of an old wooden building fronting on an alley in Iron City, Idaho. Beautiful, nameless woman I loved.

I ended the fight with Doug that night by kicking him as hard as I could in the balls. All the way to Spokane he lay in the back seat of the car, moaning and swearing at me. I drove and John sat in front with me. We drank a fifth of Scotch in an hour and a half, passing the bottle back and forth, not saying anything.

After I dropped them off, I drove to my house (my parents were gone); parked in the driveway, threw up out the car door and then passed out sitting behind the wheel.

Twenty years later, when I had dried out from drinking and I was heading out from Spokane on a coast-to-coast drive, I stopped in Iron City at 2:30 in the afternoon. The same whorehouse was still there, in the same place. I went in the alley entrance. The madam brought the girls into the waiting room, so that I could pick one. She wasn't there, but I chose one who was. I went into the room with her. She asked me what I wanted. I asked her how much a half and half was. She said that it was twenty bucks. I told her that was what I wanted. She took my money and left me to get undressed. I thought it was a different room, but I couldn't be sure. It didn't smell like wildflowers, just the antiseptic and some sugary smell to cover it up. I got undressed and looked at the scar next to my liver and at how my belly hung down and how stupid small and soft my cock was. She came back into the room and checked me out, squeezing my cock and squirting some stuff into it to make sure I didn't have clap or syph. Then she told me to lie down on my back on the bed. I did. She took her nightie off and kind of laid across part of the bed and took my cock in her mouth. I could barely feel anything at all. She was pretty. She knew what she was doing. It wasn't her fault at all.

"You been sick or something, Honey?" She raised her head up from my cock and smiled at me, a sort of pity/concern in her eyes. She held my cock between her thumb and fingers, shaking it as though she were jacking me off.

"Yeah," I said, "I've had some trouble with my liver."

"Too much partying?"

"Yeah, I guess . . . look," I said, feeling desperate, "this isn't going to work."

"You want to come?" Her eyes were earnest, the pity gone. "You want to come, you give me another twenty-five and you'll come. You're not going to get your half and half, but I'll get you to come soft in my mouth. O.K.?"

I gave her twenty-five dollars, and she left the room again. I stayed on the bed, looking at the ceiling, trying as hard as I could not to think, not to remember. Jesus, of course she was gone. Twenty years. She was married, maybe dead. Time didn't just stop, didn't come back around. There was no wildflower smell, no beautiful black hair, no wonderful taste of woman. I was just in a whorehouse in the afternoon.

My whore came back and she was right. I didn't get hard, but I came. I drove on east as far as Butte and stayed in a Big 6 motel and went to a Keno game and lost another twenty-five dollars.

* * *

And now...
And now?
And now I'm alone with the spirits in the snow in a cabin in the wilderness. Stupid Indians. Stupid Ida Greycloud. She acted more white than the white girls; homely, stolid, uptight. Why did she have a name like Greycloud if she was going to be happy being Fifth Executive in the Girls Federation in a white kids' school named for Lewis and Clark? Was she happy? Where is she now? Working as an aging token/totem secretary in some Spokane insurance office? Back on the reservation? A drunken or dead whore in some town that looks the way Spokane used to? Was she faking it all? Was she really a "Greycloud," the way Crazy Horse really is who he is? Was she an Indian and was she so scared of whites that she couldn't show it? They killed Crazy Horse—at least they thought they did—and Sitting Bull and Big Foot and hunted down Joseph and all the varieties they could find of Geronimo. Maybe she chose Fifth Executive as an alternative to death. Didn't we... don't we... didn't I... don't I want to kill every Indian we can find? Fuck them and kill them. Shake their spirits out the way a dog shakes a rat to death. I can't deal with things like this. I've built myself a fort out here in the woods and my mind is burning it down. Soon I'll be alone in the snow under the pines

at the edge of the lake, and then I'll see it all. I'll touch it. I'll hold the heart in my hands.

What heart? You kill a wild animal and then you cut out its heart and eat it while it's still hot and wet. That's what you do. It's a ritual, a ceremony. You honor the dead. You celebrate life in death. It's a goddamn harmonious circle. But that's not the way it is. Not really. If I die out in the snow on the lakefront, I'm not holding any heart in my hand. This America, this West doesn't work that way. When my friend Gary and I talked about what we would do when the Russians invaded, when we saw the cloud from the H-bomb explosion rise over the Cascades, we imagined ourselves as guerrilla fighters. But the only American guerrillas were the Indians. We thought we would take our girlfriends/wives and hide out in the woods. White men never did that in America, Indians did. Mountain Men imitated Indians. They drank buffalo blood and ate deer hearts because the Indians did. They took Indian women for their mates. But the Mountain Men weren't American White Men; they were something else. American White Men built churches, forts, schools and opened dry-goods stores; became doctors, lawyers, or loggers or big-time ranchers or farmers. They did all the science that built the Atomic weapons that ended up with the Russians dropping an H-bomb on Seattle and forcing Gary and me and our girlfriends to run into the woods. Ida—poor Ida goddamn Greycloud—tried to hide out in the American White Man's world by being Fifth Executive of Girls' Federation at Lewis and Clark High School in Spokane, Washington. Gary and I wanted to run like Chief Joseph and fight like Indians. I should have married Ida, let her be my Debra Paget. Maybe I would have if I had been older and saner and she hadn't been so big and homely. Whatever, we never thought that when the Russians dropped the bomb that the woods around Spokane would get poisoned, that the bark would fall off the trees and the animals would die and that we would, ourselves, choke on the radioactive world. We figured, like the Indians before us, like the Lakotas ghost-dancing before Wounded Knee, that God, Nature, or the Great Spirits of the world would curse and kill the Russians or the Seventh Cavalry for the crime of attacking and killing nature without the slightest pretense of a ritual, or a ceremony; for shooting people in a herd, or dropping a bomb on the innocents without recognizing how sacred their existences were. We didn't think this out. We had never even heard about ghost dancing or Wounded Knee. We didn't think of the Russians as just being anonymous parallels to our fathers, or the Elks Club, or the Kiwanis. We weren't radical, we weren't even aware that we were political; we just created our fantasy out of instinct. There was nothing mystical about it.

What the fuck, Indians weren't mystical; they aren't mystical. They're just people. When my father sold insurance to the Duwammish, they made him an honorary Indian. He got drunk with the Sachem in the tribal longhouse. So what if he was a Shriner, a Moose and State President of the Elks; so what if he shouted racism into his son's ears—he had an Indian name. That's more than I have. My grandfather claimed Indian blood—Cherokee—and he was named after Philip Sheridan, who has been given the credit for saying: "The only good Indian is a dead Indian;" and my grandfather was proud of the name, and proud of claiming Cherokee. The only thing that my grandfather was ever good at was taking care of horses, and my father used to claim that he would rather be a beachcomber than sell insurance.

Oh, Jesus. Everybody's crazy. It's not just me.

* * *

It's bitter cold today. I got up in the middle of the night, the fire had gone out and I heard a weird, low wail out in the dark. It was a dog. He was right

outside the door, freezing, hungry and skinny as hell. He's a mix—hound, husky, maybe lab. I brought him in and gave him some cheese and water. He didn't want to get too close to me. He ate and drank and then starting pacing, staying close to the walls of the cabin. He has real bright, wolf eyes. I hope he isn't feral. I want him to stay. I want to talk to him. If he attacks me, I'll have to kill him. I call him Dog, but I also call him Crazy Horse. I whisper that name at him. I want him to know that if he really is Crazy Horse, that it's all right with me. That I've been waiting for him. So I say to him, as he's pacing: "Dog. Dog. Dog. Crazy Horse. Dog. Dog." He just keeps his wolf-eyes on me and his tail low and circles around the walls. I want to ask him questions. I want to ask him where he came from, how long he's been out here at the lakefront, what he was before he was a dog. But I have to wait for that. If I just give him food and water and let him get warm then he'll trust me and then he'll talk to me.

He's been in the woods, up in the hills behind the cabin. I can smell it on him. It was deep night and he was running in the woods. There weren't even any stars out, no moon. In the dark of the woods. The simple, real forest. You travel with what you hear, what you smell, what you feel with the bottoms of your feet. If I were out there like he was what would I do? Stop and hold onto a tree? Lie down? Scream? I only trust my eyes; I need paths, trails, roads—some sort of goddamn map through the world; some evidence that someone like me has been there before me. A guide. No wonder the Pilgrims screamed when they first saw their New Eden. "Strange Beasts and Strange Men." No sign of civilization. If you walk into the woods—just into the woods with no map, no road, no trail—if you go alone, what do you find? The Pilgrims called it a "howling wilderness;" Henry Thoreau said that wildernesses don't howl; only people howl. Stand still and feel and listen—Oh, God, how I wish I could do this right now, for one time in my life do the thing as I feel it—shut your mind down, tell that busy little voice of your self to keep its fucking mouth shut, and let yourself live in the breathing, howling, crying, laughing sentient heart of the world. Let it swarm you in raucous silence; feel what you hear in your fingertips; taste what you smell in your mouth. Stop saying "me" in your mind; stop feeling "me." Allow yourself the pure brilliance of breathing in the moment. Is that what this strange, stray, wild dog did in the night? This creature who circles the room staring at me with his fever eyes? If only he would tell me.

I could tell him things. The first things I really remember clearly are all about the woods and what I called the big swamp that were at the end of the road when my family lived on 27th Avenue. I was about five when I started to wander into the woods. I would go out into the back yard to play and then edge my way through the trees on the undeveloped lots to the east of our house. There was a hill that ran down. It ended in a big dirt turn-around. The woods and the swamp began there. There was a dirt path that led off to the north—more of a trail than a road, and, at first I would walk down that path and I would hear my mother's voice and then see her behind me. She'd come to bring me back and warn me about how dangerous the woods were, and, especially, the swamp that lay beyond them. She warned me about snakes and big birds and said that there might be wolves or bears out in the wild darkness under the trees. Her warnings only made me want to go back again to the path into the forest and into the mystery of the swamp. So, I did. Day after day. She finally stopped coming to get me. She just begged me to be careful; to walk only on the path; to never go so far that I couldn't see the turn-around; and never, never to go into the swamp. Of course, I did exactly the opposite. Oh, God! Even now, if I concentrate, I can see the woods around me. The trees were huge alongside the path and the path got narrower as I walked further. At the top of a hill—I could no longer even guess where the turn-around was—it turned sharply to the east and almost disappeared. It was like a line on the ground and when I looked up I could see the tall grasses of the swamp spread out like an ocean below and beyond me. I'm there now. Now. The only sounds come from the trees, the birds and the winds in the grasses. I don't even want to breathe. I am so afraid, and yet I want to run down the hill through the forest and out into that field of grasses. Everything is so huge. Stepping into the woods, I put my hands on the trees and look up. I can barely see the tops of them and the rough pine bark feels as though it is moving against my fingers. I yell and my voice echoes back at me and I hear the wings of birds in flight. And now I'm running through the trees. There is no trail and I run around trees and bushes that are even taller than I am. I have to climb over fallen trees. I hear the small noises of squirrels? rabbits? in the forest around me. And, then, suddenly I am out of the woods. I have run into the grasses. They are way over my head. Some big cattails bend down and I can grab their heads in my hands. The ground is dry, not wet like I thought the swamp would be, but I can smell wetness around me. I am in the swamp. I stand as still as I can and I hear and feel the grasses moving all around me, above my head and everywhere I look. I can't see anything but the grasses, not even the trees. I don't know where I am. I don't know where the woods are. I have never been more afraid. I have run into the swamp and I don't know how to get out again. I am lost. I stand very still and try to think. If I stayed here I would die. The swamp is so big that nobody could ever find me. I stand there, crying now, lost in the world. And then I see, on the ground, the mark of a shoe in the broken grasses. My shoe! I turn around and focus on the broken grass behind me. Another shoe-mark and another! I am not quite six years old and I have learned how to explore— no, not explore—walk and be in the world without people. I will not die. I will follow my shoe-prints back and I will never tell anyone what I have done. And I will do it again and again, further each time. I press my face into the cattails and kiss them. Oh, to be free in the world!

That is one thing I would tell him.

Another thing I could tell him, if he would listen, would be the story of a drive I took some thirty years later, on 27th Street, down the hill past my old family house. At first I thought that I was lost, that I was so drunk that I no longer knew my way around Spokane. The street just went on and on; no dirt turn-around; no trees. Houses on either side of the street, and where the forest had been, hiding the swamp from civilized eyes, more houses. Houses with lawns and little shrubs and cultivated flower gardens and 27th running through the heart of what had been the swamp, with side streets running off, connecting the houses to the strip-mall glut that had become 29th Avenue. I stopped my car in the middle of the street in the middle of the swamp and got out and got down on my hands and felt the asphalt, pushing my fingernails into it,

trying to free the cattails and soaring swamp grass that lay buried under it. I started beating on the street. A man came out of a house and yelled at me. I looked up at him, crying, and he made a shooing gesture with his hand, "... or I'll call the cops!" he yelled. I pulled myself back into my car and drove away along 27th Street, across the swamp and when I climbed the hill on the other side, I stopped again, got out and looked back. A stupid gesture. Everything was gone. I kept on driving, out 29th to the east, to

Moran Prairie, a wide area of grasses punctuated by scrub farms and the antennas of the Spokane radio stations. Beyond Moran Prairie were the high hills separating Spokane from Coeur d'Alene Lake and the mountains on the other side of the lake. South of the Prairie, roads dipped down into the beginnings of the wheat farms of the Palouse. But Moran Prairie was gone. Housing developments ran as far as I could see, running, it seemed, right up the sides of the foothills. Something had gone wrong. I was lost. I was in the wrong place. I was too drunk; too crazy. I had driven to some strange spot in some strange town. This was my fault. I knew that because I knew that I was neither drunk nor crazy. I had gone away. And while I was gone, this world—whatever or whoever it was—had driven the Indians from Spokane and built sky bridges between stores, office buildings and across streets so that shoppers, workers or tourists need never even touch the sidewalk or street, much less the earth, with their feet; had replaced the Mint and the Buck n' Doe with ice cream parlors and fancy cafes; had torn down the railroad station and sanitized the river; and, now, also, finally had driven the birds, the squirrels and the coyotes out of the swamp and off the prairie, had canceled their world, driven them beyond the hills or turned them into broken beggars. This whole world was dead Indians' land!

So what! Do you know what that means, Dog? Dog, dog, dog, Crazy Horse, dog? Do you? I didn't do it. I was never a real cowboy. I pushed a wino down a hill and ate a whore. I was never anything more than a frightened, rootless stranger in the world. Just a kid who was scared because he was told to be, and who screeched inside with joy when he discovered he could walk into the grasses of the swamp and come back out alive. But then, I took that joy, called it being brave, called myself hunter and took my brother's BB pistol into that swamp and shot at squirrels. I, dumb little kid, took a gun into their home and shot at them because I didn't know what else to do. Do you know what I'm talking about, dog?

The dog has stopped circling the room. He's stretched out on the floor with his front paws pointing at me. He's had enough water and the cheese must have cut his hunger. His big, bright Husky eyes are focused on me. He's listening.

O.K., dog. I don't need to create a therapist in my mind, to imagine somebody sitting in this room with me; and I don't need to pretend that I'm writing this stuff down. I've got you and your strange blue eyes looking right at me. I can talk to you. I can tell it all to you. I can tell you the truth.

I'm not a kid. I've been telling you about the swamp and the woods and what used to be and I've been telling you that I went into that world and felt my heart bursting with joy and that I set about destroying the world I found and that then somebody came after me and finished the job and cut down those trees and paved that swamp and filled the land with houses and lawns and stores; and that I hate nameless them and me for doing it. But I'm not a kid—I'm middle-aged and drunk and filled with grief and staggering around the edge of self-pity. I'm running through my past looking for reasons for everything that happened.

There aren't any.

* * *

Let's do first things first, Crazy Horse. Drunk. Why am I drunk? Why am I a drunk? No. Forget the genetic stuff; forget the addiction stuff. That's all true and so is the fact that I started drinking so that I could show my father just how good I was—by beating him at his own game, out-drinking him. But the reason in my mind that I'm drunk and want to stay drunk has nothing to do with genetics or the so very obvious addiction. That "reason" is that I can create a world in my mind and I can live there no matter what is going on outside of me. Let me give you an example: One night I was sitting on my Aunt Queenie's couch and I was talking to a man standing right next to me. I looked up at him and said: "You're in the linoleum business? Well, my cousin Wally is the finest linoleum guy in the whole Northwest." He looked down at me and said: "I'm Wally." I'm not sure, but I think that he took it as a joke. The truth was that I wasn't really in that living room or sitting on that couch and I had no idea that I was talking to my cousin Wally who I had known all my life. I was somewhere else, talking to a stranger who made me think of my cousin and I wanted that stranger, whoever he was, to know that my cousin was better than he was. I remember walking into a bar one night, ordering a drink and turning and introducing myself to the stranger sitting next to me. We shook hands and then he said: "We met last night, right here, and you did the same thing. Are you funning with me?" No, of course not (although I didn't say it), I'm just making up my world as I go along. You see, dog, that's what drunks can do. You want to live in the moment, you make up the moment; you have access to an alternative world, infinitely preferable to the real world of pain and loss. If you're sober, you have what's around you. You have to act in the world as it is. Drunk, you're free of time. You write the play as you want to live it. Sober, you're cursed with memory and a past; drunk, you've pulled down the shades and locked the door, and the moment bubbles eternally. One night I went into a bar with a friend. I got up to go to the men's room. After half an hour, he got nervous and went to look for me. He found me lying behind the rear wheels of a parked car, up under the bumper. He was horrified. He thought that I was trying to kill myself. When I got up, I told him that was nonsense, that I had just been tired and thought that I would rest for awhile. Oh, dog, your eyes tell me that you wonder if things like that scare me. No, no. Never. What scares me is starting to get sober and remembering that friends of mine and I spent three afternoons following a Japanese gardener from job to job (like Gail, he'd been interred in a camp during the war, but, being older, he'd lost his business and home). His name was Takashita, spelled out on the side of his truck. We would pull up our bikes in front of the yard where he was working and scream at him: "Go back to Japan, Jap! Take a Shit a! Take a Shit a! Get out, Jap! Take a Shit a!" Then we'd ride off and wait to follow him to his next job.

That's the stuff that scares me. That's memory. That's dry thinking. The booze takes that away. What I cry about, Crazy Horse, and crying is exactly what thinking about stuff like making fun of Joe Takashita is, crying is complaining about the loss of innocence and that's all I cry about. But, who says that there was any innocence to start with? Is it just something I read about in a book? When I was nine I read Tennyson's "Idylls of the King," and in it Arthur stumbles over his Fool on the dark stairs and demands to know who was hiding there and the Fool says: "It is your Fool, and I shall never make you laugh again." That frightened me.

When I was a little boy, my mother used to take me to the duck pond in Manito Park. She would tell me that the duck pond was my brother's favorite place in the world when he was little like I was. I never went there with my brother, but I loved the pond in my own way. There were so many ducks that I thought that it must be the very center of Duck World. I could go down to the edge of the water and they would swim towards me and quack. They wanted bits of bread, but I didn't know that. I thought that they were saying hello to me. I grew to love all of Manito Park. Before I had a bike and could go on adventures out of the town, even after I had discovered the Swamp and all that I could do there, Manito held magic for me. Not only was the duck pond there, but also there were blocks (that must have seemed like miles to me) of woods that were filled with secret hiding places; huge rocks that I could climb on; and paths that led into the wonderfully fragrant darkness of the trees. With Manito as a start, I always looked for parks (I sometimes think that I thought of the Swamp as a wild park). In Seattle, there was huge Woodland Park with its zoo and wild Carkeek with the wind from the Sound roaring in the valleys beside the creeks; in Walla Walla there was manicured Pioneer with its own duck pond and its night darkness where we could park our cars and make-out and drink beer. When I got to New York, I found Central Park. I loved to walk in it, day or night. I didn't know enough to ever be afraid. One afternoon I was in the woods behind the outdoor theater. There were little hillocks of rocks and trees and heavy underbrush. As I looked around, I saw what looked like a couple lying in a small clearing behind some bushes. I focused on them and discovered that it was very definitely a couple. They were fucking in the afternoon, in a lovely September afternoon. I stood silently and watched them. Then I heard a grunting noise off to my right. I looked and there, sitting on a rock staring at the same couple I was looking at, was a bedraggled black man, holding a fedora hat in his hand and masturbating frantically. In the compass of my glance, he groaned loudly and ejaculated into his hat. He spurted and spurted and spurted. And then, finished and holding his hat in both hands like a supplicant at some sort of altar, he turned and looked at me and smiled broadly. It was as though he felt we were somehow sharing in what I had just seen—the couple fucking and him masturbating—that we had done it all together. I didn't know what to do. I do know that I gave him a short smile in return, advertent or inadvertent, and I know my heart was pounding. Was I frightened or was I excited? Oh, dog! Oh, Crazy Horse! I don't think I'll ever know the answer. I looked back at the couple. They were still caught in their idyll. And then I ran. Out of the park and all the way to a little bar on 74th and Columbus.

Innocence? No. Were my precious sensibilities violated? No. Was Nature soiled, damaged, destroyed? No. As I sat on a stool in the bar, I told myself that all over the world there are and were people fucking in parks and men jacking off watching them, just as, all over the world, there are men fucking cattle and sheep and horses, and young boys eating whores in whore houses or pushing winos down dark hillsides, or Indians dying in alleys. Ah, Shit. I am a part of it all.

That's one of the reasons I drink. But you don't care. You're a dog—or maybe you're a shape-changing Indian named Crazy Horse and you're appearing to me in a vision.

* * *

Whatever he was, I gave him more cheese and a stick of pepperoni that was in the bottom of my food bag, filled his water dish and watched him eat and drink. I was tired. Remembering made me tired. I needed to stop thinking for a few moments. Just rest.

Easier said than done. I'm too nervous now. I'm almost sober and I have less than half a quart of vodka. I have to save it. But, now my father's after me again. When I was fourteen, I wanted desperately to be important, to be popular. I wasn't. I was playing cowboy and Indian games with kids who were three and four years younger than me. I was afraid of my house when my father was there, and, at night, when our next-door neighbor took care of me while my mother accompanied my father to the private clubs he drank in. Places with names like The Early Birds or, simpler, The City Club where they had booze, food and slot machines that were illegal in Spokane except in private clubs. My mother didn't drink, so she plugged nickel after nickel into the slots, while my father drank and blathered with the men he called his friends. She went with him—I found out later from my brother—because he was getting himself a reputation as a womanizer while she stayed home with me, and so she went out to the clubs and the bars to save her marriage and to show Spokane that he had a wife. So, I was left with baby-sitters. By the age of fourteen I was getting used to it, in fact, by the fall of my fourteenth year, I was left alone, period, staying with my brother while they went south to Palm Springs for four months. But, while they were home, I was afraid. I didn't like it when my father didn't recognize me when he came home and knocked me down the basement stairs by accident. I didn't like it when he and one of his drinking buddies sat in the little summer house in our back yard and he kept ordering me to get a bottle of I.W Harper for him from the house, and when I went in and my mother would tell me to tell my father that he couldn't have it. Back and forth I went like a ping-pong ball, until I ended up hiding in the dark behind the garage and listening to them yelling at each other. It was much better for me when they left me alone, first with my brother and then simply alone, staying in the family house with my brother coming down from his house or stopping on the way home from work to check up on me. It was better, too, because then I could start drinking myself to give my big, fat fuck of a father a nice little surprise when he came back to Spokane.

But that fall, before they went South and before I found out that I could be popular by raiding my father's liquor stock to give to kids I wanted to be my friends, or by having beer delivered by the local grocery store and charging it to our family account; before all that, I tried to cure my loneliness by joining DeMolay. It was a mistake because the DeMolays were strictly coke and peanuts guys, but so was I when I joined, and, anyway, it turned out to be a short-lived mistake. I have my father to thank for ending it for me. I went to meetings and training for a couple of months and then they had a dinner/initiation that was for new members and their fathers (if the fathers were Masons, which my father was). I was afraid to even let my father know about it, but my mother convinced me that I should invite him, that it would be good for us as father and son. So I did. The Masonic Temple in Spokane was right next door to the Elks Lodge. My father and I went in to the Temple together. As soon as he saw the set-up for the dinner, he whispered to me that he was going next door to Elks, and I could come and get him there when it was over. It wasn't that he suddenly had something against the Masons; it was the fact that there was no bar. I knew that, although he didn't say it. I knew what he wanted to do. I went through the dinner, mumbling some sort of apologies for the nametag next to me, and through the initiation. It was nothing special and I recognized that; it was boring and awkward and almost foolish. I was sorry that I had gone through it. And then I had to go next door to the Elks to get my father. They had a door guard sitting at a desk just inside the big wooden doors. He asked me what I wanted and then told me to wait at the desk while he got my father from the bar. The entrance hall to the Lodge was a huge marble-lined dome with doors leading off it to the bar, the lodge-meeting room, the rooms for out-of-town Elks to stay in, the dining room and the swimming pool and gymnasium in the basement. My father had been Grand Exalted Ruler of the Spokane Elks Lodge and I had never been

in the building before. There was nobody else in the lobby and I could hear the voices from the bar. When the door guard came out of the bar he had hold of my father's arm. But he wasn't quite strong enough, because my father slipped out of his grip and fell to his knees on the marble floor, then he pitched forward onto the heels of his hands and looked like a baby trying to crawl. The door guard left him there and told me that he was going to step out and hail a cab and that I should try to get my father up on his feet again. I couldn't do it. He slapped at my hand and said, "Mind your own god-damn business, you little prick!" The door guard returned with a cab driver. Between the two of them they got my father up, out the door, down the stairs, across the sidewalk and into the back of the cab. He sprawled out on the seat, so the cab driver told me to sit up front. It was a Yellow Cab, and my father wasn't too drunk to notice that. I told the driver where we wanted to go, and my father started to yell: "Salsbury's the shits! He's a son of a bitch! The shits!" I didn't know it at the time, but Salsbury owned the Yellow Cab Company in Spokane and he had refused to buy insurance from my father. After a couple of minutes of yelling about Salsbury, my father passed out. I sat, wearing a goddamn sport-jacket and tie for the first time in my life, silently next to the driver, just hoping to hell that he could drag my father out of the cab and up the front steps of our house and down the hall to his bed. I never went back into either The Masonic Temple or the Elks Lodge again.

What did I want my father to do? If he thought Salsbury was "the shits," would I have been proud if he would have called Salsbury out and had a gunfight at the intersection of Howard and Riverside at high noon? Would that have been better than yelling and cursing and passing out in the back of a taxicab? Did I want that kind of Wyatt Earp/Wild Bill Hikcock stuff from him? And my mother a little frontier wife running into the street in front of Mode O'Day to stop the carnage? I don't think so. But, when my friends and I got cars at sixteen, we started dragging the gut on Riverside and one time my friend Art called out a carload of guys from North Central and one of them got out and fought Art right in the middle of Howard Street. It was the afternoon of a school holiday and the sidewalks were filled with kids, shoppers and businessmen heading in and out of their office buildings. Art beat the shit out of the North Central guy and people on the streets cheered. There were no cops to be seen. Art jumped back in our car and we drove off, shaking our fists in triumph out of the windows and giving the finger to anybody who looked at us. A lot of people gave us the finger right back. We felt like Rodeo Kings. After that we would drag the gut a lot—in caravans of three or four cars at times—but we never had a flat-out fight in the intersection again. There would be calling out and then fights set for Comstock Park or Moran Prairie at night. Some of those were bloody, but nobody ever used weapons, a guy named Jay once got his faced smashed up and teeth knocked out because the guy he was fighting got him down and beat his face on a tree stump. But that was as bad as it ever got.

You know, dog—you're listening again, I can tell, maybe it's the violence—when I walked out on DeMolay and all the mystic junk of their initiation; when my father showed me a different way of dealing with loneliness, I joined the Social Club group at Lewis and Clark. All the important people were in Social Clubs. The Girls' clubs were like sewing circles without the sewing. The girls would meet and talk and plan parties. If you wanted to be Old Mythic West about it, you could imagine them planning church socials or picnic basket auctions. But the boys' clubs were quite a bit different. They had initiations. For a full semester, an initiate had to supply chewing gum to any member who demanded it at any time, had to do any member's bidding (run errands, pull stupid stunts), and, one night a week, at the club's meeting, he had to be prepared to be hacked as many as thirty times (one for each member, if the member so chose) with a wooden paddle that had the club's crest on it. After a semester of this, the club's actual initiation took place on a Saturday night between semesters. It would usually be on Moran Prairie (although I went through one in Comstock Park that actually brought the cops out); the initiates were to make bunches of paddles (20 apple-slat; 20 1/4 inch; 10 1/2 inch; and one 2 inch thick "memory paddle") and wait at the Modern Maid coffee shop to be picked up by members. When they were picked up and stuffed into the back seats of members' cars, they were blindfolded and told to be quiet. Once the cars reached the prairie, they were formed in a giant circle—like the old wagon-train circles on the Plains—the initiates were dragged out, still blindfolded, their paddles were taken away from them and their hands were tied behind their backs. Then the members, with stacks of paddles beside them, formed into a circle themselves. One member got the blindfolded initiates lined up and started them running. They ran around the circle of members, being hacked continually. Supposedly the members were trying to hack the initiates on the buttocks. But, with the initiates running and stumbling because they were blindfolded, the members hacked them on the back of the legs, on the sides of their bodies, the arms, shoulders, even on the head. For a while, if an initiate dropped, he was pulled up and forced back into the running circle. But, after about a half an hour, initiates were pulled out of the circle one by one and taken aside. They were told to hold onto an arm that was held in front of them and bend over. Then they were beaten until either they passed out or hitting them broke their memory paddle.

That done, and still blindfolded, initiates were

grouped together and members moved among them, stripping their bloody clothes off. Then they were covered with molasses. Then with feathers. And then each initiate was given a bottle of horse liniment and instructed to rub it all over his balls. It hurt like Hell— and yet, when I think of the burning of the liniment, I remember one 14-year-old friend of mine, whose balls hadn't dropped yet. The members made him bend over and poured the liniment up his ass. Then, beaten bloody, molassesed and feathered, balls on fire, the initiates were left alone on the winter prairie. The members warned them not to take off the blindfolds until all the cars were gone. And, in the cold January night, naked, feathered boys, crying in pain, staggered off in the dark to find their homes. Each one alone, in his own misery, pain and shame. When I got home from my first initiation, my mother caught me trying to sneak in the back door and down to the basement, she shrieked and wanted to call the cops. I told her no, got downstairs, cleaned myself in the shower and fell on my bed, holding my balls in my hand and crying. So. Is that what the Indians did? Was that a rite of passage into manhood, into becoming a member of the tribe. If so, what tribe? We talked about that after we'd been through it. When it was happening, we were too scared to do anything but cry.

When I was a senior I was president of my club. I was supposed to be in charge of initiation. But I didn't go to it. At least at first. I got a call at the Modern Maid. It was an emergency. I had to get out to Moran as fast as I could. We were in trouble. When I got there I found out quickly what trouble meant. Larry and Neil, two wild friends of mine, were running the initiation. They were drunk. It was a May afternoon and we had decided to have the initiation early. But it turned out that it was too early. Larry and Neil had decided, since it was light, to have the initiates run blindfold races. One of them had run into a barbed-wire fence and had passed out from the shock. Three other initiates were throwing up. Neil had the idea that it would be fun to have them eat fresh cow pies. John had called me from a pay phone outside the Moran Prairie grocery store. By the time that I got there, the guy who had run into the barbed-wire fence had come to. He was sitting on the ground, dizzy and bleeding. He still had his blindfold on and his hands tied behind his back. The other initiates were covered with cow shit and, still blindfolded and tied, were either throwing up or rolling around on the ground coughing and crying. It was too much for me. Too stupid. I took a piece of fence-post and hit Neil as hard as I could behind his knees. He pitched forward to the ground, yowling, and I said "Eat some of that shit yourself, bright eyes!" Larry saw me with the fence-post and took off on a dead run for his car. John and I set about untying the initiates' hands. We took their blindfolds off. Some of them rubbed their eyes with the cow-shit still on their hands and set about crying all over again. We checked the guy who had run into the fence, untying him and taking his blindfold off. He wasn't cut bad, just welts across his bare chest and arms. He was lucky it wasn't worse, since he'd been running naked, he could have cut up his belly and his cock and balls. It was a fucking mess. A dozen, naked, crying, shit-covered fourteen and fifteen year-old kids; me and John, all of seventeen and eighteen, and Neil, bitching and rolling around on the ground holding the back of his legs. I'm sure that I felt sorry for the kids at the time, but all I remember clearly was worrying

about getting them all cleaned up and out of there before cops came, and figuring out some way so that none of them or their parents would tell either the cops or the school officials. We didn't have any water, so we made them put their clothes on right over the caked cow-shit. Then we piled them into cars, mine, John's and goddamn crazy Neil's. We told them that the initiation was over and that they were members of the club now. And the stupid little bastards were happy. They wanted to shake hands. Nobody was going to get in trouble. Our new club-brothers were grateful. They belonged. They didn't know what I did, or, that left alone a little longer, Neil would have tried to kill the whole bunch of them. He was that crazy. He fed off the violence of it all, like he was drinking some sort of madness out of the ground on the prairie. I saw his eyes before I hit him and they were like bits of burning coal. Neil got into some bad trouble on assault charges that summer and was given the choice of a jail term or going into the army. He went to Korea and I never heard what happened to him. Years later, when I read about the My Lai massacre in Viet Nam, I thought about Neil and that May afternoon on Moran Prairie.

It's easy to talk about Neil and his craziness, but we were all involved in everything that went on. When I hit Neil with the fence-post, I wanted to break his legs. Confronted by crazy brutality, I went crazy. John Wayne hummed a tune in my head.

Give me men to match my mountains. When I was a kid everything told me that the West demanded big men. Tall, bigheaded, heavy through the shoulders, long arms and legs, narrow waists and big hands. Heavy, meaty hands. In his movies, John Wayne used to pick up smaller, slighter men by the back of their collars or the seat of their pants; grab a belt or a shirt and throw a man away from him. I remember him picking up a two by four in his big hand and hitting another man in the face with it. Wayne was meant to be the Man of the West. Never a real family, never a love that lasted—separate, isolate, alone. More than town tamers, Wayne's characters were meant to be land tamers. Above, beyond, superior to the law, whether he wore a badge or not, the Wayne character brought order to the land through the power of his presence. I never liked him. I was afraid of him, as I was afraid of my father; but I hated him for the inflexible shallowness of the morality he represented, for the cruelty in his single-mindedness, just as I hated my father's weakness. In Wayne's characters I saw contempt for those who were different, as though difference were indicative of weakness. I didn't like people who felt that they could change the world by grabbing it by the belt and tossing it aside. And yet I knew, god-damn-it, that the same attitude had somehow been bred into me. No matter how much I might want to be like Henry Fonda as Wyatt Earp, all gentleness, reason and understanding and yet ready to act—not picking a fight, yet not running in fear—I knew that the urge to destroy was in me. It was in all of us. I don't know what it was. Fear? Breeding anger? What was there—what is there—for us to be afraid of? My mother told me that if I said the word nigger around a black person that he or she would kill me. That made me afraid, but later it made me angry at my mother, just as my father's anti-Semitism made me angry at him. When, as little kids, we saw cowboy and Indian movies—for instance, when we saw Errol Flynn as Custer massacred by Crazy Horse and Sitting Bull—and then we saw "our" Indians, ghettoized, dirt poor and drunk on Main and Trent, or, went to the reservations and were told that they were like prison camps, did we feel cheated because we could no longer "win the West" by fighting and killing Indians? That the West had been "won" and filled with neighborhood grocery stores, little beauty parlors like the one my mother went to on Grand at 30th taking me with her when I was very young and sitting me in a chair by the window where I was given comic books to look at, and downtowns with little office buildings, filled with lawyers, dentists and insurance salesmen like

my father and stationery and department stores and movie theaters. The Storekeeper's West with taverns for the Indians and the Cowboys pushed off to the side of peaceful, progressive commerce. Is that all that what we were mad at? Is it that simple? Did the "niceness" of our small-town civilization make us want to hit each other with fence-posts, or pour horse liniment up each other's ass-holes, or roll rich Catholics' cars down hills at night to watch them crash in the park? When Warren, Pat and I picked up the wine-soaked bum in Seattle and threatened to kill him and then dumped him in the Arboretum, would we have felt better had he been the CEO of Boeing or the Mayor of Seattle? I think so.

Oh, dog! Dog, dog, Crazy Horse. You want to go out. I've been rattling on at you and I can tell that you want out. For good? Or just to piss? Look out that window. See the snow come down? See how heavy it is on the ground? O.K., o.k . . . . Out it is.

* * *

Now he's gone. And the snow is getting heavier. When I stepped out, I couldn't see the sky. There won't be much more of this. All that's left to eat is some cheese, crackers and three more of the pepperoni sticks. A bottle of water. At least the pipes aren't frozen so I can drink the lake water that's pumped up and use the toilet and flush it. I have less than a pint of vodka left. I have to save it. There's a problem there. I've been maintenance drinking, holding myself steady of the edge of the madness, but I'm beginning to feel the nerves of withdrawal. God, I hope the dog comes back. If he's here maybe I can control the shaking inside. I need to be able to think, and if I start to shake in my mind, I won't be able to. It's happening now. I am repeating myself in my head. Simplify! Simplify! Count. 1,2,3,4,5,6,7,8,9—oh, oh, oh, dog, please come back! I see him in my brain and I see the other creatures of the world. I see cats, and mice and rats, the monkeys from the zoo and zebras, and the coyote I saw in the woods once, and the baby rattlesnakes I chased into milk bottles once when I was six years old—I see them clearly—and the frogs I would flush out from the porch on the house on 27th Avenue with the garden hose. I see them too—god, it seems as though there were hundreds of them, and I would flush them out and run, laughing, chasing them under the house. No people. I don't want to see people. Just frogs and the baby rattlers that a neighbor lady said could kill me, and later, swimming among the fish at Silver Lake with my eyes open, holding my breath and sending schools of tiny fish racing as I touched the rocks on the floor of the lake. All the creatures in the world. The deer in the woods that come down to the lakeshore to drink. I've been close to them. Stand quiet, hold my breath and I can savor the delicacy of their bodies, their silky smooth movement. I can almost smell them. I see them in my head. The points of their ears; the long graceful jaw-lines; noses wet in the twilight. If I could burn my brain out, jettison my memory and live among the creatures of the world . . . if I were able to do that . . . but, all I have are those memories. If I could fly. If I could open the door of this cabin, step out and then, with strong eagle's wings soar above the pines and firs free into the heart of the blowing snow. There would be no past, no other human being's words, no life or death holding me; my talons and beak would tear at whatever fabric called itself past, or family or meaning. Oh, Jesus! Oh, God! I stay where I am. It is snowing. I am almost out of vodka and of food. Crazy Horse, the dog, has left me. I am tired of remembering, because each memory brings me closer to self-pity, or into a cloudy anger where I want to rage at . . . what? . . . is it everything that has brought me to this point? Do I want an answer for why I am whatever it is I am and the world is what it is? Christ, I'm like a drunken Job daring the Voice to come out of the Whirlwind. But that's not what I want. I want the dog to come back and be a shape-changed Crazy Horse and take me in his arms to the world that was this world before an ax felled the trees that became the wood of this cabin; where I can, so simply, just smell, hear and taste the world of the creatures of the universe. That's what I want. But, first—and maybe that's all it is, first—I have to remember everything and tell my story to myself; my voice, my world in my mind. I have to see everything as clearly as I can. I don't need to understand, I just need to try to see.

*   *   *

When I was nine, my parents started leaving me for the summer with my uncle and aunt at their little farm in Edmonds. My parents would travel to Elks' Conventions in different eastern cities, as my father worked his way from State President of the Lodge to various national offices. When I was twelve, they took me with them. I was with my mother in the day, but I spent each night alone in the hotel room. And I would wake up when I smelled the stench of the alcohol as they came in late at night. But, for three summers I stayed in Edmonds, safe from things that I didn't want to understand. It was there that I would follow my grandfather around and it was there that I taught my cousins the Lord's Prayer; and it was there that, after dark, when we were supposed to be going right to sleep, that I put my imagination to work and told my younger cousins stories.

They called them "Igga" stories. For me they were free-range adventure stories in serial form, with material picked up from comic books, movies and the world we lived in and had heard about. The heroes were Dan Druff, a down on his luck private detective; his sidekick Ferdie Lizer; and a hunch-backed servant named Igga. Dan was smart, Ferdie was funny and Igga had super-human strength. The villains were Blackie and the Gas-house Gang (who lived in the sewers of Tacoma); Flash Bulb, an evil genius, whose head would light up every time he had an idea; The Scoutmaster, the self-styled "meanest man alive," who wore shoes with five-foot spikes on them and had turned every kind of camping or hiking tool into a deadly weapon; and Icy, a man made completely of dry ice, whose touch would mean instant death. Dan, Ferdie and Igga had some help themselves in trying to fight all this malicious evil. There was the Priest who could throw the knives he carried in a harness on his shoulder as fast as anyone could shoot a gun, he never said anything save the phrase "I hate your guts." And there was the Sparkler, dressed in an Uncle Sam suit, who cried out "Happy Fourth of July," as he fired Roman Candles and threw Cherry Bombs; and there was the Swordsman, a Frenchman, who used his swords as expertly as the Priest did his knives. Finally, there was Hicky Go' Burp, an ultra wino, whose chief weapons were throwing up and a propensity for dramatically prodigious bloody noses.

The stories were violent and as graphic as I could make them. They were a mixture of things I knew, comics, cliffhanger movie serials and Doc Savage stories. If there was any meaning to them, it was that the world was in danger. Flash Bulb, Blackie and the rest were constantly waging attacks on nature; not only wishing to control people and society, they wanted to destroy the world. The Scoutmaster, the first villain I created and the one I disliked and feared the most, only wanted to hurt little boys. What I gave my cousins and myself in my stories was a solid grounding in fear. The heroes were not as powerful as the villains and were in constant danger. They escaped desperate situations; they never solved anything or brought themselves safety. For instance, when Blackie and his gang caused Mt. Rainier to erupt, Tacoma was saved from the lava flow only because Hicky had a nosebleed that was so gigantic that it blocked the flow. It was pure luck, an accident. Dan was a terrible detective. He and Ferdie were constantly walking into traps and being beaten and tied up. Once they were about to be killed by the Scoutmaster's spiked boots, and were rescued at the last moment only by the strength of Igga, who found them and held the Scoutmaster's foot in the air while he untied them with his other hand. As I remember now, I don't know why I told those stories to my cousins. I was afraid of the world that was bigger than I was and I was afraid of the adults who lived in it. I was, during the time I was telling the stories, saturated with the myth of Robin Hood. I wanted my own outlaw band that would rob from the rich and give to the poor; I wanted my own Maid Marian, just as, when I was six I had wanted a Wendy to go with my Peter Pan. I didn't know why. I just thought it would be better to be an outlaw—but not, from the stories I knew, Jesse James or the Dalton Brothers—maybe an Indian. Maybe Cochise, or Joseph, or, even, Crazy Horse. I can't remember the details of the stories very well. I just remember, almost viscerally, what it was like to tell them, how I saw the characters in my head, and how I saw their world. And I remember how my stories scared my little cousins. Maybe that was why I told them.

There were no Indians in the stories. Yet, the heroes were not at all a part of the social fabric that we were taught to respect. If they were "grown-ups," they were nothing like the adults we were supposed to take for models, nothing like what our parents told us responsible people were. Dan and Ferdie were losers, living low-rent lives in a seedy part of Tacoma; Igga was an inarticulate hunchback, lifted directly from a

Frankenstien movie; Hicky was a street-corner wino; The Priest was hardly a man of the cloth, he threw knives and never said anything save "I hate your guts;" The Swordsman loved to run people through with his sword; and the Sparkler was only happy when crying out "Happy 4th of July," and detonating his deadly powerful cherry bombs. Those were my heroes and night after night they were locked in mortal, brutal combat with a Scoutmaster, an intellectual {Flash Bulb}, a gang of gardeners {Blackie and his Gas-house Gang}, and a man of ice. What were they fighting over? Control of the land. Confusion. My heroes and my villains lived in a shadow world that I created. If their names, titles or jobs might make one think that they were a part of society, their behavior quickly disabused one of that notion. There was no reason why The Priest should be a hero and The Scoutmaster a villain, save for the fact that The Scoutmaster and his cohorts acted first and against the interests of The Priest, Dan and Ferdie and the rest. And, maybe that was it. So goddamn simple. Just Cowboys and Indians. The Cowboys, armed and brilliant, came to take the land; and, the Indians, seeming to be weak and disorganized, fought back. And, in my stories, the Indians won, or, at least, survived to fight other battles. The Scoutmaster was so hideous to me because he knew how to conquer the wilderness. He had the tools and Flash Bulb's brilliant strategies. Dan and Ferdie had only Igga's crude strength. My villains could make Mt. Rainier erupt; my heroes could only save the world by accident, and, even then, only temporarily. The country they all lived in was the West, the underbelly of the world my parents and aunts and uncles lived in, or claimed they lived in; it was my version of the Wild West, before the land was tamed, the Indians destroyed and the goddamn wood and mortar and brick towns built. Basic battles, more akin to the fights of packs of beasts, than the way my family and my teachers would describe the battles that Won The West.

Now, for some reason, I see my Aunt Mina. I only saw her once, when her family found her on First Avenue and cleaned her up for her mother's funeral. I thought, seeing her with my child's eyes, that she was

beautiful. She had the most beautiful, fierce blue eyes I had ever seen. She was a street drunk, living off prostitution in flophouse hotels. She had two children, taken from her at birth by her sister and farmed out to other families to raise. She was a whore. The first beautiful whore I ever met. My father was a drunk, his brother was a drunk, one of his other sisters died of liver failure in a rain-filled gutter on 15th NE right next to the University of Washington, his mother scrubbed floors and washed other people's laundry until she was seventy-five—a big, ham-fisted, broad-shouldered woman who would drink thirty beers a day, but Mina was a whore, and we couldn't talk about her. My father "did business" in his brutal way and was praised and envied by his family; but when Mina gave a lonely sailor a blow-job in exchange for a few drinks and a night's sleep, she was just a whore. Her sister could fuck her married boss silly until he dumped her for a younger woman, but she dressed in women's business clothes, and Mina was just a whore. Oh, Pop, won't you tell me what's wrong with Mina. "She's just a whore."

Mina had nothing to do with the stories I told my cousins. But I think of her—abandoned, smiling her sweet, kind, beautiful smile at some stranger in a bar—whenever I start to think about the "wildness" of the West. She could have been the heroine of every story I ever told.

Evelyn was my aunt who fucked her boss. She was also the one who died of liver failure and lay in a gutter next to the U. of W. in a miserable November Seattle rain. She was the baby of my father's family, the littlest sister. She lived with her mother until the mother died; then, the affair with the boss and her job in the insurance agency ended; she lived by herself, cheaply, in a house that was paid for, spending only on drink. She idolized my father. He scorned her. He sent her money and only referred to her as "Evelyn the Beggar." Uncle Art was my father's older half-brother. He was a sailor. That is to say that he was a career Navy man who worked in an office in San Diego. He had a little mustache, a harridan for a wife, and, two months after his retirement, he died from an aneurysm he suffered sitting, drinking, next to a motel swimming pool. He taught my father to swim at the age of six by tossing him off the end of a dock on Lake Union in Seattle. Art tossed him and walked away. My father thought it was a wonderful thing to have done; he claimed it taught him never to trust anyone before it was too late and he was old enough to get hurt by other people. When he got drunk, he used to tell clients the story, to let them know how tough he was.

Oh, what the fuck? They're all dead now. All, except Violet, the oldest. Violet, the only one who didn't drink. Violet, who left home in Seattle at 15, went to San Francisco and married a rich man, 35 years her senior, and when he died, married his younger brother, and when he died, married the brother's business partner, and, with each marriage, got wealthier and wealthier, so that now, with all the husbands dead, no children or grandchildren, Violet sits in her old age atop a San Francisco hill, cared for by servants.

And me? I sit here waiting for a wild dog to return from the winter night of the lake, trying to tell myself stories from my past; trying to withdraw from the alcohol without turning my memories into hallucinations. And I think about telling stories to my cousins when we were children and, for no real reason save anger and pity and love for Mina, I think about my father's family. Boy, did they ever stumble when they crossed the Cascades. The Swedes found the ocean they needed, but my grandfather was killed by a bus when he got off work as a night watchman at a reservoir; and his wife, after 60 years of scrubbing other people's floors on her knees, got to drink her diabetic self to death. Ah, the white man wins the west! What cheap shit that is. Who am I to be sarcastic about their lives? I am what they were. I like to think that I am different; that I am blessed with a self-awareness that enables me, at least, to know a sense of loss. But, I am as much a stranger here as they ever were. As my brother said, I am "a Swede down from the woods on a Saturday night." And yet, Swede that I am, I know no more about the woods than I do of the towns that replace them. I drink, like they did, to numb myself to existence. My father was so goddamn afraid of the world that he had to drink to control his shyness, and it drove him crazy. From a scared kid, he turned into a brute. I am afraid as he was. I am not a brute, but, like any other Westerner, I could easily be a killer. Violence sits at the center of my fear.

Lost in the goddamn woods.

I remember once at Loon Lake, in high school, when a bunch of kids were staying in cabins. "Having stags," we called it. The girls stayed in one group of cabins and the boys in another. Everybody met in the evenings at the general store on the lakefront. It had a dance floor and pinball machines and the guy who ran it made hamburgers and hot dogs. One night, as I was walking back to the boys' cabins late and by myself, I saw a girl I knew slightly up the hill heading to her cabin. I called out: "Gilkey!" She turned, anticipating something. I said: "God, you're a whore!" She said: "Thanks a lot!" and turned back towards her cabin. I don't know why I said what I did. There was no reason for it, save awkwardness. Later that week, at the same resort, I got caught with beer in my car. I had bought it at a country general store ten miles away using fake ID. When I was caught, I tore up the ID, but told the deputy sheriff where I had bought it. He took me there and made me confront the owner. The owner brought his wife out and his teen-age son. The owner begged me to tell the truth, that I had used the ID; he said the fine would put him out of business. But I had gotten rid of even the bits of paper the ID had been on, and I didn't want to get into worse trouble than I already was in, so I stood firm. The owner's son looked at me as I lied and said: "I'm going to find you. And I'm going to beat the shit out of you. I'm going to kill you!" The store was closed and the son never found me. And I wasn't even charged with possession. Sheriff Biddle said that he figured I had learned a good lesson. He didn't want to put a city kid in jail.

When I was fifteen I got a crush on a girl named Anne. She was my age and was, I thought at the time, beautiful with large, full breasts. It was her breasts that drew me to her. I had never seen anyone my own age who looked the way she did. Anne was going out with a kid a year older, a round sort of guy that my friends and I referred to as "Porky Bob." Porky Bob had a car and he smoked and drank—stuff I was just beginning to experiment with—he thought he was a big deal. He was buddies with a couple of mean, tough doctors' sons. Two guys named John who had a lot of spending money and the time, desire and means to intimidate and beat up other kids. They were both seventeen and both of them had tail fin Cadillacs for their cars. The rich kids in Spokane were always the worst. Because they were rich, they figured nobody could ever touch them, and they had free reign to do whatever they wanted to whomever they chose. What they usually did was violent and mean. They showed off by hurting other people.

One night Anne had a party at her house. She invited me, Gary and John. John was the only one old enough to have a driver's license, so we went in his father's car. At the party, Anne and I kind of messed around a little. I wanted to kiss her so bad. But I didn't even try. Just talked and kind of touched each other on the hands and arms. She was, after all, Porky Bob's girl and he was right there, along with his bastard doctors' sons' friends. When John and Gary and I left, we saw Porky Bob's car parked about halfway down the block. I said: "Let's fuck him up." We went down to his car. We took off the gas cap, and while one guy watched, took turns pissing in his gas tank.

The next afternoon, Gary and I were in the Modern Maid, when one of those big tail fin Caddies pulled up. It was dark-haired John's and he was driving, with him across the front seat were Porky Bob and blond John. Both Johns bolted from the doors of the car and into the Maid. "C'mon, you little fucks," dark-haired John said as he grabbed me by the arm and blond John grabbed Gary, "we're gonna take you on a little ride." They shoved us into the back seat of the tail fin and Porky Bob said: "People who piss in gas tanks get pissed on." All three of them laughed. We started up Grand and dark-haired John said: "We're gonna have a little trip up to High Drive." High Drive was the road along the top of the South Hill. There weren't many houses there, just some fancy places right on the edge and lots of fields. Gary and I looked at each other. We both figured they could do one of two things with us, either pull off alongside one of the fields and beat the shit out of us, or push us over the edge of the Hill, where we'd have about a 20 foot drop into some scrub pines. Or, they could do both. Beat the shit out of us and then throw us off the edge. Basically we knew that they could do anything they wanted to, because they were bigger than we were, and stronger, and we were afraid of them. We drove up Grand with them talking and laughing among themselves and Gary and I sitting terrified in the back seat. At 29th, blond John said: "Whoa! Stop now! There's Pickerel!" Tom Pickerel, who was in the same year at school as the Johns, was raking in his front yard. Blond John jumped out of the car and grabbed Tom and threw him against his front porch. When Tom tried to stand up, blond John hit him, and then hit him again and again, until Tom was just lying on the walkway leading to the porch. Blond John got back into the car and said: "That'll teach the son of a bitch." Dark-haired John and Porky Bob laughed. Nobody ever said what it was that Tom was supposed to have learned. When we got to High Drive, we turned right and sped past the big houses that were on the crest with their big valley views and then turned right on a dirt road and headed between two fields. Porky Bob turned around and leaned over the front seat and said: "O.K., you little pricks, why did you piss in my gas tank?" "We didn't—I didn't . . . ," I said. "Don't lie to me, you fuck! You want to come back down off this hill, you tell me the truth!" Porky Bob's face was red. It made him look even fatter. "I tell you, we didn't do it," I said. "Ah, fuck it!" he turned back around in the seat. "Stop it here," he said to dark-haired John; "Let's do 'em." Dark-haired John stopped the car and he got out and opened one back door and dragged me out, while blond John opened the other and grabbed Gary. This time Porky Bob got out too. It was really dusty, and stopping the car so suddenly had raised a big swirling cloud. They pulled us out of it and got us standing on a hill. Just then, out of the dust, came my friend John's car. He had seen the other Johns and Porky Bob pick us up at the Maid and had followed us all the way. John got out and said: "I stopped on the way and called the cops, you guys. I told them there was some trouble up on High Drive. They're on their way." Porky Bob said: "He's bullshitting! There's no cops gonna come up here." Dark-haired John said: "I'm not about to fuck around with it. Too many people here already. Let this be a lesson to these little fucks. Look, one of 'em's pissed his pants already." He pointed at the front of Gary's pants. They were wet. Dark-haired John and Blond John headed back to their tail fin, Porky Bob sputtered a minute. He pointed at me. "You stay away from my car and you stay away from my girl." Then he went back to the tail fin and they left.

Anne broke up with Porky Bob when she heard what had happened. I asked my friend Betty Jo to tell her that I really liked her. I went up to Anne's the next week and spent a whole evening with her, hanging out in her back yard and walking around the neighborhood. I kissed her three times, once with our mouths open. I felt her breasts up against my body. The next day Betty Jo told me that Anne really liked me, and had told her, Betty Jo, that I could do anything I wanted to with her. I didn't know what the hell it was all about, but I got a boner and jacked off just thinking about what her breasts would look like bare. I couldn't even imagine her cunt. I went up to

Anne's on Saturday. We went out walking and talking and holding hands and touching each other. And then something crazy happened. I said, "Let's get married." And she said, "O.K." We were fifteen. I kissed her and cupped one of her breasts in my hand. And then we went back to her house and I hot-wired her father's car that was sitting in the driveway and we got in and took off for Coeur d'Alene, where we figured we could get married. Her father ran after the car as it was heading away. We got out of town and on the Coeur d'Alene highway and almost to the Idaho border before the cops caught us.

No big deal. A cop drove the car back. My brother was waiting outside Anne's house and took me away. Anne went inside with her parents. The next day Anne was shipped off to a Catholic girls boarding school in Walla Walla. I saw her twice more. Once at a party when I was eighteen, where she told me that if I'd convert and be a Catholic that she'd go all the way with me; and once, when I was twenty-one, and back in Spokane from college, a couple of guys I knew from the Park Inn Tavern and I went a seedy theater downtown, and put on 3-D glasses and looked at Anne's bare breasts in a Russ Meyer movie. It seemed that she had dropped out of the Catholic Church routine. Her breasts were incredible.

* * *

Hey, Mr. Shrink man! Hey, Mr.-Dr.-Shrink-in-my-head, come on out and talk to me. I need you. My dog's gone. Crazy Horse has gone out into the snow. I need to talk to somebody. I need to know why I remember that story so well and why I went from thinking about my father's family to it. I need to have you here. Ah! Thank you. You don't have to say anything, just so long as I can feel your presence. All right? All right.

*   *   *

You see, I don't think that that story's about the two Johns and Porky Bob and the trip to High Drive. I don't think it's about my lying; or my friend John's timely arrival; or Gary pissing his pants. Sure, the two Johns could have done everything but kill us (maybe even that if they'd thrown us off the right point on the hill) and not gotten into any trouble. Our parents were afraid of their parents. Their parents were, as my father put it, "prominent people" in Spokane. They were rich doctors and my father sold insurance and Gary's dad owned a little grocery store. If we'd gone home beaten bloody and told them who did it to us, they would have told us to forget about it and get cleaned up. They were that kind of afraid. So, the story's not about that. It's about Anne. And me. It's not about Anne's breasts either, that's just stuck in my mind because of seeing her naked in that goddamn 3-D porn movie. I had only kissed one girl before Anne, and yet, after a little kissing and touching, I hot-wired her father's car and took off to get married. Sure, you're right. I know. I was only fifteen years old. But, getting married? I also thought—and told Anne—that after we got married, we would head up into Northern Idaho, to Spirit Lake and then we'd ditch her father's car, build ourselves a little cabin on the lake and live off the land. But Anne turned Catholic and then she turned whore in goddamn 3-D porn. I thought my Aunt Mina was so beautiful and I thought that Anne was so beautiful, shiny long blond hair, beautiful face. But, goddamn it, I see her now, two nipples in 3-D, me in my glasses, and my drunk friends laughing and snorting next to me in the dark, stinking movie theater. My frontier bride. See how crazy this all is. Why should I care, so many years later, why should I remember with such violence in my heart? Did I get stuck with some of my father's virtue? Mina's a whore. Anne's a whore. Anybody's a whore if they get caught. But, you and me, Pop, we can fuck anything we can grab, drink as much as we want to, and, if we get caught, we can name-call and blame everybody else. As if somebody actually gave a shit what we thought. I sometimes wonder if we hadn't, in our different ways, been so desperate and careless, life around us would have been a little better. I know that, at fifteen, I really wanted to go to Spirit Lake with Anne. I wanted to lie down naked with her and marvel at the beauty of her body. But I didn't want us to be two young, white kids from the South Hill of Spokane with a stolen car. I wanted us to be Indians from before the white man came to the West. I wanted us to be able to live off the land. I wanted the tribe to rejoice in and celebrate our love. I didn't want her god-damn banker father to send her away to a Catholic School and I didn't want my father to insist that, after Anne was gone off to school, I go up to her parents' house and apologize to them. How the hell can you climb to the treetops and reach out and touch the moon, if you're crawling on your knees apologizing to the very people who destroyed the land around you? No wonder I wanted to let rich Catholics cars crash into each other; no wonder I wanted to go to a whorehouse so badly.

After Anne's parents shipped her off to Walla Walla, I got friendly with a girl named Sharon. She was a quiet, pretty girl who liked popular music. She and I met a couple of times at a record store downtown and sat in a booth and listened to 45's. After the second time we did that, as we were walking to the bus stop, she told me that we couldn't start hanging out together because her boyfriend was getting out of Monroe and would be back in Spokane by the weekend. Monroe was the state reformatory and only hard-case juvy offenders went there. I didn't even ask her what her boyfriend had done to get sent there, but I knew from the way she was talking that it was something pretty violent and extreme. I just thought knives and guns. I wasn't stupid, so I said goodbye to her and made a vow to myself not to even look her way at school.

A bunch of us fifteen and fourteen year olds went downtown to the Desert Hotel Coffee Shop a lot after school to have cokes. I say the age specifically because after age 16, people either had cars or knew people who did, so there was no more walking downtown and taking the bus. At least with the kids I knew. About a week after Sharon told me about her boyfriend coming back from Monroe, I was sitting in a booth at the Desert with a couple of my friends, when an older guy I didn't know came over and asked me my name. When I told him, he said he was Bruce and that he'd like to talk to me privately. He put his hand on my arm and I saw that he had a snake tattoo that ran from his wrist to his elbow. I got up and went with him. I still don't know why, but I did. My friend John started to get up, but Bruce motioned for him to sit down. Bruce sort of ushered me out of the side door of the Desert and, once we got outside, he grabbed my arm hard and steered me up the street and down the alley behind the hotel. When we were about halfway down the alley, he spun me around and hit me hard in the face. I went down to my knees and he kicked me in the balls. When I fell the rest of the way down, he started kicking me in the side and in the back. I was holding my balls. He had really hurt me. Then he said: "Look at me, you little prick!" He pulled a switchblade out of his pocket and flipped it open. "I'm gonna cut off that little pecker of yours and give it to Sharon as a present." Monroe! I rolled away from his feet and managed to get up as he swung the knife at me and then I was off and running. Running as fast as I could, I was out of the alley and heading up the hill, back towards school, towards home. I didn't look around until I'd run the half-block to the next street. Then I checked over my shoulder. No sign of Bruce. He hadn't followed me.

All of this when I was fifteen. On my sixteenth birthday, I got my driver's license and a car. It was a big, old boat of a Chrysler. My father had driven it for three years and then passed it to my brother for five more, and then it was my turn. It had 150,000 miles and smoked oil out the exhaust like a diesel, but, to me, it was freedom. The first night I had it I drove north out Wall Street, a right-of-way street, with a 25 mph speed limit, and screamed with joy when the speedometer hit 100 as I roared through an intersection. I was a man and I had the fastest horse in the tribe. Within a month, I had two taverns where I could buy beer without ID, and John and I had been to the whorehouses in Wallace, Idaho. My parents were gone all winter to the desert, and, in the summer, they would be off to Elks' Conventions, or they would go off to Canada on "fishing trips," where my father would have a guide motor him around while he got drunk. I had the house to myself. I had the town to myself. I had a car, and even if I didn't have any money, I could charge gas at a local station. I supported myself by buying beer for other kids and charging them extra. My brother checked by the house every once in awhile, but he really didn't want to be bothered. He had young kids of his own and didn't have time to be my father. So. I was an actor, and I had rehearsals and performances; and I had a girlfriend who would sit in the car with me in the dark, under the trees, and let me touch her all over her body. She would never touch my cock, or let me pull her panties down. But, mainly I had freedom and I had friends, a gang of friends, a pack, a tribe. I had been really a loner, or a guy with one or two friends, but the car brought me friends from everywhere, and we could go anywhere. We even figured out our own version of my father's "fishing trips." My friend John's parents had a cabin on Twin Lakes that they never used. It had electricity but no phone and the heat came from a big open wood-burning fireplace. My friends could tell their parents (and I'd tell my brother) that they were going to the cabin for the weekend. Since we were all "good," "respectable" young men, no one doubted that we would fish and, if it were warm enough, swim and have a "good" time. On one of our fishing trips to John's cabin, we headed north out of Spokane after school on Friday, and drove up, skirting Indian Country to the Canadian border. We got to the border about midnight, and since we were on a small state road, there was just a gatehouse at the border where they did what customs inspecting was required. It was closed and there was a wooden bar out across the road. I backed up the Chrysler and took a good run at the bar. It snapped right off, and we drove into Canada.

We drove for a couple of hours and then came back, we didn't want to get caught in Canada when the border opened at six in the morning. On the way back south, we slept by the side of the road for a while, and got to the town of Chewelah about 11:00 in the morning. We decided to "take the town," see how much we could shoplift and outright steal without getting caught. There were four of us, me, John, Gary and Larry. Larry was the best at stealing. He was a little guy, but he had a nervous kind of courage that made him dare to do things that we were too afraid to try. We had big, loose shirts on, so we got beer, cheese, cookies, bread and crackers from grocery stores (we ended up with four cases of beer); we went into a jewelry store and Larry got away with four watches; we got fountain pens out of a stationary store and three desk calendars. Each store we hit lost something to us. Out in the street, John said: "So many Indians come into this town from the res, they'll blame all the stuff that's gone on them. They'll clean 'em out of the taverns." We took toys and knick-knacks and shit like that from the dime store. Larry even took the mailbox off the front of the bank. On the way back to John's cabin, we started getting itchy about the state patrol, so we threw all the stuff we had stolen out the windows of the car, except for the beer and a couple bags of potato chips. "Those 'skins will get it anyway," John said, as he tossed the watches out the window and over the edge of a steep hill. We were driving right alongside the boundary of the Spokane Reservation.

We also used John's parents' cabin as a base of operations for late-night vandal raids on Hayden Lake. Hayden is a small lake north of Coeur d'Alene and about half an hour's drive from Twin. Hayden Lake Village is an enclave of houses, most of them just summer houses, belonging to rich Spokane people (and some used-to-be Spokane people—Bing Crosby had a summer house there); it has a golf course, a clubhouse with, when we were kids anyway, a fancy restaurant and slot-machines. It was private and exclusive. It was mostly Catholic, which for us kind of doubled the stakes. At night, the enclave had a gatehouse, but no guard. We figured that the residents didn't want to know how drunk their teen-age kids were or what time they got home. Also, across the highway and south towards Coeur d'Alene from the Village were three motels. Everybody called them Cheater Motels because the main customers were residents of the Village fucking each other's spouses. We hated the Village, the people who lived there, and the social pretensions it stood for. So, we would go in after midnight with shovels and rakes to chop up the greens on the golf course and rake sand over the torn turf. We would steal hoses from people's yards; bicycles; name and address signs that were posted at the end of driveways; mailboxes; anything that was loose and that we could carry. We'd load the car and then drive the stuff to someplace like Rathdrum and dump it in a vacant lot. We never kept any of it. All we wanted to do was irritate the rich bastards; make them hurt a little bit; inconvenience them; make those jerks get red in the face and curse in anger; maybe they'd get drunk and beat their children some more. That's all we wanted.

    A lot of times we just got drunk and took girls out to the cabin, had them put on John's mother's swimsuits (she had about a half-dozen that she kept at the cabin), go swimming, and then try to get the girls to take the swimming suits off. Nobody ever scored that way, but it was fun to try.

    Having a car, having my house in Spokane with my

parents gone most of the time and having John's parents' cabin made us feel free. Once, when John and I were sophomores in high school and I was newly sixteen, we drove to Coeur d'Alene town (in Idaho it was legal to drink at 20) and sat in a bar talking to the bartender about the dangers of under-age drinking. We told him we were sophomores at Washington State College in Pullman instead of sophomores at Lewis and Clark High School. We didn't feel sixteen; we didn't feel like sophomores in high school. We felt free in the world. But, the next day, I got called into the vice-principal's office about cutting school. He shut the door behind me and demanded to know who had been with me the day before. It turned out that we had made a bit of a mistake, before we went to Coeur d'Alene; we had driven into the West Valley High School parking lot. We had spun out, done 180's, honked the horn and given the finger to anyone who cared to look out the window at us. Somebody had got the license plate on the car and traced it back to my father, and thus to me. So the vice-principal was plenty pissed-off. He threatened me with expulsion if I didn't tell him who was with me. Then, he hit me. Right in the face. Hard. So hard, in fact, he knocked me up against the door. He hit me again. I didn't know what to do. He told me he would give me five minutes in the hall to find the person I had been with, and, if I had nobody at that time, he would throw me out of school. It's all so simple. John was waiting for me in the hall. He went in and told the vice-principal that he had been with me. He didn't get hit. We each got two weeks of a half-hour detention after school. We knew the student who was supervising us, so we never served a minute after the first day. Later, I became friends with the vice-principal's son and I asked him why his father hit me so hard. He said: "He doesn't like you. He thinks you're a smart-ass." I always wanted to hit him back. I used to fantasize about hitting him with my car. Catch him just as he came off the curb heading for his car and bounce him off my front fender.

* * *

Oh, Doctor! Oh, Doctor! My mind is twisting me all up again. I keep hearing the word "whore." Why?

Why did I call Gilkey, the girl walking to her cabin at Loon Lake, a whore? Did I think she was? Her brother was an ass-hole; did that make her a whore? Mina was a whore. Was Anne? Did pretty, blond, fifteen-year-old Anne turn into a whore by showing the world her twenty-one-year-old tits in 3-D? I think of Ida Greycloud, and see her as a secretary or a whore, maybe both, like my aunt Evelyn, never any other possibilities for Ida. Women in the West are whores—like Mina, Mitzi Gaynor, or the women in the Ashford, the Ritz, or Iron City; or they're virgins—like my high school girlfriends or Doris Day as Calamity Jane; or they're compromised good women who are married and have to fuck in order to have children, as my mother told me. Sex was, for those good women, a duty, something to be endured. This is not about them. It never was. It is and was me—in my head. It's the goddamn fantasy. Part of it's Henry Fonda as Wyatt Earp. He was so calm, so rational, so kind, such a gentleman and, yet ready at a moment's notice and capable of the most extreme violence. And part of it's Jimmy Stewart in *Winchester 73*, a good man avenging a terrible wrong and committing fratricide in the act. Men of the West. Alone. Moral. Knowing the land; knowing how to touch it; how to live on and with it. Ready to destroy evil if confronted by it. Ready, also, to accept and return the love of a good woman. These were not the men who took the land from the Indians and slaughtered them; they were closer to Mountain Men than shopkeepers. They were what I wanted to be. If I could not be Cochise, I wanted to be the white man who married his daughter. At times, driving at night with my friends, I became a different kind of Westerner: One of the Daltons or the Youngers. We would drive the wrong way down one-way streets, with cars parked facing us on either side, and, with three of us swinging tire-irons out of the open car windows, smash as many anonymous headlights as we could. We called it "playing polo." Or, we would tail-gate older men driving alone on narrow two-lane blacktop roads; honking, flicking the headlights; pulling up to touch bumpers; driving along side and yelling, then dropping back. We did this until the frustrated, sometimes terrified, driver would pull off to the side of the road, or turn down a side road. Once we followed a guy all the way to his house, far out in the country down a maze of lonely, dark roads. He jumped out and screamed at us: "I've got a gun in the house, you bastards!" Then he ran as fast as he could up the front stairs to the door. We shouted, laughed and drove away quickly, just in case he did have a gun. Outlaw. Lawman. Avenger. All of them in the fantasy. Much of my life an amateurish Western Movie. And the women. In a fantasy, a Westerner needs whores and schoolmarms. Maybe Gilkey was a whore. I doubt it. But, when tongue-tied and forced to make a decision, I labeled her as one. I didn't know what else to say. But why?

You answer that one for me.

* * *

There was a Grange Hall north of Spokane out the Little Spokane at a place known as Nine Mile. It was built like a church, and maybe that was what it had been when it was put-up. It was old, particularly for buildings around Spokane. It probably dated back to the 1890s. It was covered with rough-cut shakes and shingles, which, when it was dark, made it look like some kind of frontier ghost house. One night a bunch of us had been drinking and riding freight cars, or, what we called riding freight cars. We'd pull up our cars at a railroad crossing when a long freight was coming through. The train was just coming out of the yards in Hilyard, so it was going very slowly. We would grab a hold of a side ladder on a freight car and ride it through the crossing, then jump down, run back over the crossing, grab another ladder and repeat the process. It was exhilarating as hell, particularly when the train started to pick up speed. Being a little drunk made it all the more exciting. When the train was gone, we were filled with a kind of mad energy. We got into our cars and drove out to the Grange Hall. It was something we'd wanted to do for a long time. There weren't any houses or any buildings anywhere close to it, and we had all been by it lots of times when we were heading out into the country towards the Indian Reservation. We knew when there were meetings there and when it was dark. This particular night it was empty. It sat there in the middle of a big, dusty field that was used as a parking lot, looking as dead as the settlers who built it. What we intended was a raid. The city boys were going to make a strike against the fort of the 4-H Future Farmers of the countryside.

We started by taking rocks we'd picked up out of the trunks of our cars. They were good, big rocks. Then four of us threw them at the windows. Four windows shattered with what sounded like one crash. We started tearing off the long shake siding. It was old and filthy. We tossed it into a pile.

Gary, John and I had started trying to hang out with a guy named Art. He was big, like a weightlifter, with thick, muscled arms. He didn't look like a teen-ager and he didn't act like one. He barely went to school and had been kicked off the football team. He didn't care. He drank a lot and loved to fight, particularly with older town guys who worked in construction or at the lumber mills. We wanted him to think we were his buddies just in case the two Johns or Bruce or somebody like them wanted us. If you're going to fuck around, it's good to have a really hard-case guy on your side. That's what Art was. He was stupid as hell, but that didn't bother us. All we had to do to amuse him was give him beer, talk about fucking and find things for him to destroy. That's what he did with the front door at the Grange. He destroyed it. He hit it three times with his shoulder and then kicked it once. It fell off its hinges. We went into the building in a smashing frenzy; breaking the legs off tables, beating chairs to pieces on the floor, turning over file cabinets. There were papers everywhere. Art literally tore the toilet off the floor in the bathroom and a geyser of water shot up. Then John said that he'd had enough. "Let's just burn the place down and get out of here," he said and started lighting matches and setting the papers on fire. We threw the broken tables and bits of chairs onto the fires he was starting. The Grange Hall was so old that it was like a stand of dry, dead trees. It started to blaze up in spite of the water spurting out of the broken toilet. We ran out. By the time we got in our cars it was blazing like a giant

bonfire. We knew that even though the Grange Hall was isolated that it wouldn't take long for the fire trucks to get there, so we headed off fast and drove onto the Indian Reservation. We knew we could circle through it and come out about fifty miles north of where we were. There was nothing, not even houses, on the part of the Reservation we went through. So few Indians were left that they were all clumped together in government housing in two small groups. The only Indians driving at night would be drunk. Good scapegoats.

We were right about it all. We got home and the

Grange Hall burning made the papers the next day. The State Patrol blamed unknown Indians for setting the fire. That made us feel just fine, because we knew that if the Indians could have, they would have. Eighty years before, they sure would have. So, we did it for them. That's what we said to each other, anyway. But, we were laughing when we said it. What we really felt was fuck the Indians, and fuck the cowboys, too. There was such joy in destroying. That was our reward. And, the love of our girlfriends, if we had them. We never told them what we did when we were out "on the range." We kept things separate. Good boys, nice and respectable from good families. My girl's parents thought I was dependable, with "a good future." She, Sandy, trusted me. She let me touch her, smell her and put my hands on her lovely bare breasts. But, no further. She was a good girl. Yes, we would get married when we were older, and then we would do all the things married people did. And, it was fine with me—the waiting, because I wanted to marry a virgin, and, because just around Coeur d'Alene Lake, through 4th of July Canyon, nestled in the Kootenais, were the whorehouses of Wallace, Kellogg and Iron City. You were never supposed to kiss a whore on the mouth, and that was fine with me too. Here is my Virgin; here, my Whore. I burn down buildings; I get A's in school.

* * *

I'm so fucking tired. I want the dog to come back. I don't want to have to keep remembering. It's all the same anyway: Indians and whores; drunken Cowboys fighting; and Nightriders, out to pillage and hurt. Wherever I am, whatever I'm doing, it's what's in my mind. My West. Diminished versions of the myths and fantasies acted out almost as rituals in the midst of the fading radiance of the Nature that the shopkeepers and town-builders felt hide-bound to control and destroy. I'm all of them, inside me, struggling not to become the town clerk or schoolteacher that is my destiny.

All the western movies taught us, and, before them, the western stories, the dime novels. In all the little western towns, the saloons were filled with cowboys, wanderers, gamblers, sojourners drinking, maybe gambling. And, after the drinking, and, maybe, the gambling, fights—with fists or guns—and/or whores in the rooms above the saloon. That was the West we were told about. Indians were either broken, drunk or Christianized, or they were threats in the outland that, like the sheep or cow-raiding coyotes, had to be eradicated. Respectable people in the towns were cowards. The ministers, shopkeepers, civil servants had to be protected, if not by the law in the form of a strong town marshal or sheriff, then by some right-thinking, compassionate cowboy who was expert with a gun. None of us wanted to be respectable. Neither did our immigrant or children of immigrant parents. The Swede, the Bohunk, the Chink were forced into the woods or to a sweating servitude laying the tracks of the railroad, and when they staggered into town on a Saturday night, they were not ready to practice civil obedience. They had nothing of the land; they had nothing to protect. When the railroad tracks were laid, the storekeepers and clerks, emboldened now by bankers' suits and owning real estate in new cities like Tacoma and Seattle wanted to get rid of the Chinks. They wanted to send them back to China, but they didn't want to do it themselves. They enlisted the Swedes, the Bohunks, the shanty Irish and all the rest of the disenfranchised white trash and pointed at the yellow skin and the slanty eyes and told them the Chinks would take all the work away from them because "they'll work cheaper than Indians." They tried to load the Chinese on boats, but the boats sank, and most of the Chinese stayed, hiding now in Chinatown ghettoes behind stacks of White Man's laundry or serving Chop Suey and Chow Mein in tank towns throughout the west. When the Wobblies tried to organize the Swedes and the Bohunks, telling them that they had the right to a living wage and the right to own property, those clerks in bankers' suits, called in the Pinkertons and the troops and killed anyone who objected. No wonder immigrants' kids like my father and his friends, uneducated and filled with energy, drank away their lives in 20th Century cowboy saloons; sold insurance to Indians and tried to cheat the government in any way they could. Kill or jail the Indian; drive the Chinks into ghettoes; never let the Niggers in; and give the white trash second-class citizenship. Let them own small houses; let them do business with one another; let them move the furniture; let them sell and service the cars. As the West was covered over with towns and the pavement of towns, those who didn't own it worked for those who did, sometimes not even knowing it. Cowboys on a ranch. They did their jobs and then got drunk, fought and fucked whores. If they were white.

And then their children came. The sons and daughters of those sons of the immigrants who had worked their way into owning car dealerships, or lumber yards, or moving vans or insurance agencies, and they went to college and sold out their fathers, if they could, grabbing their own bankers' suits, sleeping and working with the enemy; trying like hell to pass themselves off as potential ranchers, not just another bunch of cowboys.

And for some of us it never worked. Fuck them all!

* * *

Would I wear lace panties, women's underwear, in the woods? Yes, I would, if I could even find the woods. God, I think sometimes of those guys, my grandfather and his brother in the newly named Glacier Park, in the midst of that ancient, virgin {to the eyes, hands and plans of white men} forest. No paved roads, no cars, just people building huge log structures, with the railroad spur being the only real evidence of white civilization. What was it like for them? What did it smell like? I can smell these woods here. Did it smell like that? Or, was it a fresher, greener smell? What was it like before them? What was it like for an Indian who wandered into that place in the mountains, in the forest? What was it like when he touched the trees? That's what I want to know. My grandfather and his brother cut trees down, sawed them, pulled their stumps out of the ground. These woods here smell of pine and fir, but also, on bad days, they smell of smoke, of creosote from the mill in Coeur d'Alene and the oiling the logs get up the St. Joe after they're cut down. For Hand-axe Pete and Rip-saw Joe there was the oil smell from the railroad and the smell, almost like the smell of burning, of the lumber being sawed. But first. Before that, here, or in Glacier, or on the beautiful, wild Olympic Peninsula, did the smell of the forest overwhelm the senses? I know that deep in the rain forests of the Peninsula, the smell is intoxicating, a wonderful drug to the senses. Even now, when you go far enough off the road, you disappear, covered over, awash in green. The West was once like that: Desert or forest, wild and natural; throat-parching dry or deep cold soaking wet. It is now something else, and one finds reality only in protected or overlooked pockets. The natural earth.

You know, I don't even know if that's what I'm talking about or thinking about. Does some nutty naturalist yearning for a world I've never seen lie under the stories I keep telling myself? Am I that crazy? Crazier than my grandfather and his Northwest Passage dreams? Crazier than my father who said he wanted to be like an Indian while he voted to keep Jews out of Manito Golf Club? I don't think so. My father had that desperate immigrant need to make something of himself, to be successful no matter what the cost. He felt as though he lived in a world of enemies. He thought that people with formal educations looked down on him and all he could do was shout and swear them down to his level or below. "Salsbury's the shits!" He was a rough, crass, destructive man. He didn't mean to be. He courted my mother by telling her that he wanted to be like Jesus. But, he acted all his adult life like a cornered animal. He bared his fangs and growled and hissed until he could feel comfortable enough, enough in control to cuff the person he was with around, playfully, like the biggest, strongest cub in the litter. He could make fun of people so long as they couldn't make fun of him. An enormous, fat man, he would call his friends, those who fawned enough in his presence, "Fatso," so long as he knew that they would never call him fat. Fear was the key. His fear made him comfortable only around those who were afraid of him. It may not have been what he wanted, but he didn't have a choice, no more than does a cougar or a bear driven into a dead-end canyon. My grandfather, my mother's father, was my father's opposite. He was not afraid, because he had no competitive desire. I hated the money my father made. It was never very much, but I felt that he got it at the expense of other people. I didn't think that he really earned it, to my mind he beat it out of those he did what he called "business" with. It was intimidation money. He hit people with words and with the volume of his voice. He ran roughshod over people; he might just as well have been John Wayne hitting the man in the face with a piece of fence-rail. Even when he was sick and on the way to dying in the last hospital, he tried to fire the male nurse who tended him at night. His doctor asked me if I knew that my father was insane. I told him I did. That was true. I had known it since I was a child.

But he is dead now. As is my mother. As are all of my grandparents. And my aunts and uncles. And I, cut off from the world of the living human by choice, sit, no longer drunk, in the near dark of a lake cabin in the depths of winter, trying to use my mind and my memory as ways to my own salvation. And I remember. It seems, at times, as though I remember everything. It's all disordered, out of any sequence. It all comes from feeling. Erratic, crazy feeling. I start to cry and I stop myself by remembering violence, and then, before I start to beat my fists against the walls, I think of some heart-breaking loss or humiliation and I swerve back towards tears. Of course, none of it makes any sense. It is just what I do as an alternative to doing nothing. I am not ready to die yet.

* * *

George Shedd wanted to kill Jim Finigan. We were freshmen in college, and Shedd was one of the most brilliant among us. Shedd advocated fucking sheep over any other kind of sexual activity, and convincingly defeated Frank Wilbur in a debate over the relative merits of sheep versus cows. Shedd was also brilliant in math and physics—that scary kind of icy brilliance some scientists have, those who say, "Of course we can construct an atomic bomb"—and he hated Jim Finigan. He claimed that the Fin was so dumb that "he couldn't find his dick in the dark." Shedd wanted to wire Fin's bed and set up a remote control system so that Shedd could flip a switch in his room and electrocute the Fin in his sleep. He got as far as attaching a wiring structure to the bed when a resident counselor caught him and made him undo it. Shedd was frustrated, and the Fin lived. All the Fin wanted, in a town filled with whores and whorehouses, was what he called "Free Ass." Shedd was right: the Fin was stupid. In fact, he was almost crippled by his stupidity. We made fun of him relentlessly and he thought of us as his friends. I still wonder what it actually was that the Fin thought about. When you looked at him, his eyes were blank, almost reflective like a dog's when light hits them a certain way. He grunted or shouted instead of talking. And he wanted free ass. He was like a male dog constantly sniffing a bitch in heat. Dean and Steve and I decided to try to profit from the Fin's lust. Dean's girlfriend, Amey, said that one of her sorority sisters, a girl named Jane Eland would, as Dean put it "fuck anything that touched her." It sounded crazy to us, but it also sounded like a potential gold mine. I'd figured out that what the Fin meant when he said free ass, was just non-whore house sex. With him, it wasn't the money, but, in some crazy way, the principle of the thing. The Fin had lots of money—his parents were rich Canadians; his father was an "oil baron"—and he would spend it, so long as he didn't have to give cash to the woman he fucked. I think that all the poor, stupid, screwed-up bastard wanted was some love and affection. He wanted a girlfriend. A mate. Well, instead of that, I made a deal with him (always my father's son—"doing business"); he would buy us a keg of beer and we would deliver into his hands a girl who would fuck him for free. I became a pimp. Dean became a pimp. Amey became a pimp. Amey got Jane. The Fin bought a keg of beer. Dean and I loaded it into the trunk of my old Chrysler, and carloads of us headed out the road along the river up into the wooded and wild foothills of the Blue Mountains. There was a patch of land where the river bent, leaving the farms and heading up into the clusters of summer cabins in the woods. Nobody really stopped there at all, because the water was wild and rough and there was just a small bit of a sand and gravel mix beach, and then heavy forest. We parked by the side of the road and got the keg down under the bridge that crossed the river's bend. We didn't need a fire because it was late spring and a warm clear night. There were eight of us, six guys and two girls. Plus the Fin and Jane. I didn't count them as being in the group.

    The Fin rode out with Dean and me. Just us three and the keg. The Fin was so excited that I didn't want him to jump all over Jane out in front of the dorm. The whole business we were up to was illegal as hell. It made me dizzy. We were all under-age, carting a keg of beer that was bought with fake ID out to a drink and fuck party. Dean talked to the Fin all the way out to the party spot. The way the Fin was twitching and the wild, glassy look of his eyes made me wish we'd muzzled and cuffed him. When we got there it was just dark and the light came from the stars and the three-quarter moon. We were the last to arrive, so everybody was clammering for the beer. Dean and I starting setting up, but the Fin wasn't interested in any drinking. He spotted Jane with Amey and went straight at her. He mumbled something to her, and then, like some goddamn beast dragging its prey into its cave, he grabbed her arm and headed into the woods. We tapped the keg and everybody started drinking. Maybe five minutes passed and we heard somebody shout in the woods. It wasn't the Fin and it wasn't Jane. Then we heard a crash and the Fin howl. The Fin staggered out of the woods and onto the tiny beach. His head was all bloody. Behind him, whacking at his back with a tree-limb was a guy named George. He was a towny who had heard about a drinking party at the tavern where we got the keg. "This bastard was fucking some bitch in the woods! I'll be god-damned if he's gonna get pussy and I'm not!" He hit the Fin on the head again and knocked him into the water. Dean and I went into the river to pick up the Fin. George went back into the woods where Jane was. Everybody else just stood there, stunned. The Fin was O.K., but he had no idea of where he was. Dean and I got him into the back of my Chrysler. He was moaning softly: "Free Ass." We got him to the hospital and he got bandaged up. George got Jane. Our friends got the keg of beer. The only thing that

Jane got was fucked by a cruel stranger. The Fin flunked out of school at the end of the semester and we never heard anything about him again.

I was there, at least for that part of the Fin's life, so I know it happened. In fact, I made it all happen. As for the further adventures of the Fin, I can only guess. I think he went back up to Vancouver. Maybe his parents were smart and shut him up in the basement or attic. Maybe they saw that crazed, reflecting gloss over his eyes, and, maybe, they took care of him, maybe even sent him to a doctor and got him some sort of treatment. Or, probably they didn't, or, there was no treatment, and, probably the Fin wandered the night streets of Vancouver; raping women when he could, getting beat up and rolled, until, probably, he finally got his head bashed in bad and somebody dumped his body in the Frazier River. As I say, just probably, and we all know what a lousy predictor I am.

If the Fin was nuts, or retarded because all he thought about was ejaculation, but ejaculation in one, specific way, then Gordon "Jack-Time" Elias was nuts in another way. "Bug-eyes" Rigway had a pet monkey that masturbated itself to death. Elias was like that monkey. He couldn't leave his cock alone. He had a roommate in the freshmen dorm. That didn't bother "Jack-Time." He jacked off with his roommate in the room. He jacked off with his dorm room door open, so that anybody walking down the hall could see him. He sat in the back row corners of classrooms and jacked off there, covered only by his jacket. He jacked off all the time. He knew his nickname and was proud of it. He even called himself "Jack-Time." A group of six or eight people, say, would be sitting at a table in the Student Union Building and Elias would get up and say: "Well, it's time for a little "Jack-Time." If the Fin paid the price for his lust by being beaten by a treebranch and knocked into a river, then Jack-Time paid his dues as well. He beat himself into a triple hernia. He had to be carried down from his dorm room to an ambulance. He couldn't walk. When they put him in the ambulance, his fly was open and his little cock was lying there like some wounded small animal. Jack-Time never returned to school. Like the Fin, he lived in our memories as some sad signpost of stupidity.

Free Ass. Jacking-off. Jim Allenton got married while he was still an undergraduate. He got a dose of the clap from a town girl at his bachelor party and gave it to his bride on their wedding night. I fucked a black whore; Warren fucked an Indian. We both wanted to fuck an Asian. That song goes on. We talked about fucking so much that we made ourselves think about it all the time. In our minds, if not in our deeds, we were rapists. Sons of our fathers. Don't even try to tell me that Lewis and Clark kept their peckers in their pants. As my friend John would say: "Ah, so much Indian poon-tang!" The Fin was no better nor worse than any of the rest of us, only dumber and more blatant. All the white boys want free ass. At least that's what we thought at the time. Did you fuck her? Did you finger-fuck her? Did you get bare tit? Did you get covered tit? Did she touch your cock? Did you take it out of your pants? Did you come? Did you get the "rocks?" Did you—did you—did you—did you? Tell me all about it? Jack said, "I really love Marty," as he sniffed his middle finger while we sat in his car in my driveway. Oh, tell me all about it!

Why are we so fucked up?

We could be nice boys. Nice young men. Nice older men. We had some social graces. Our mothers raised us to be members of the righteous community. But, when we looked into mirrors and stuck out our tongues, they were forked; our eyes were mocking; our ears strangely pointed. It's still the case. I feel that doubleness now. The minister walks down the street with a hard-on. He carries a gun in his pocket. There was a joke I learned in grade school that I thought was very funny. It was about Pastor Fuzz. It went like this: On a cold, snowy night Pastor Fuzz and his secretary, Miss Bendy, had been working late. When they were done working, the Pastor suggested that he walk Miss Bendy home because the weather was so foul. They walked together, Miss Bendy holding the Pastor's arm so that she wouldn't slip. When they came to the bottom of a hill and tried to cross the street, they both slipped and fell down. Pastor Fuzz fell on top of Miss Bendy. The ground was so icy that he couldn't get up. Each time he tried he slipped again. He was bouncing up and down on Miss Bendy, and she cried out each time he slipped and fell back down on her. While the Pastor was trying to get up, Officer Brown came by and saw them on the ground under the streetlight, Pastor Fuzz bouncing up and down. "All right, buddy!" Officer Brown said, "That's enough of that in public!" Pastor Fuzz looked up and said, "But, officer, you don't understand, I'm Pastor Fuzz!" "I don't care if you're in up to your armpits," the officer poked the Pastor with his night-stick, "you can't be fucking out on a public street. It's off to jail for you." I loved that joke. And, every time I thought of the minister at the Presbyterian Church where I went to Sunday school and where my mother taught Bible Studies, I thought of him as Pastor Fuzz. I knew that everybody thought the same way that I did. When I was a kid, before I knew what sex was, I used to like to go out into the dark at night and shoot at imaginary Indians. If I were walking down one of the dirt roads that were around our house, I could see wild, war-painted heads rising from the brush or peeking around a tree. I would fire at them, using my finger as a pistol. When I discovered sex, I added rape to my fantasy. I could jack-off ferociously, picturing Debra Paget in her made-up Indian beauty as Cochise's daughter. My mind would let me rip her beaded leather clothes and discover—Oh, God! Just thinking of it now makes me want to jack-off again, because under that buckskin were all the secrets of the universe, if I could just see her naked body and it were truly an Indian body and I could shoot my jizz all over her I would be immortal! Crazy bastard, crazy, and still crazy! It's all still there. If you are not born to it, if you are not part of it, then kill it, rape it, force your will upon it! All of it was real, the land, the trees, the animals, the birds, the rocks, the dirt and the People who lived with it. If it isn't mine, fuck it! And, I knew that the prissy, thin-lipped minister at our Presbyterian Church felt exactly the same way. He *was* Pastor Fuzz.

* * *

I need to be quiet. I feel as though I have broken something inside of me. Just a little stillness. When I start to shriek inside, I'm not sure if it is some kind of real emotion or just the d.t.'s. I'm out of vodka and I may be starting to sober up, so I have to be very careful. I want everything to be real, even the memories. If I start to make up stories it will be because I'm seeing things. And I'll be goddamned if I want my life to end in a hallucination. So. Careful and slow. When I think about that wino in Seattle—picking him up, terrorizing him, and then dumping him in the arboretum—he, what we did to him, why we did it all, it becomes part of a pattern. Sobering up, I'm not shocked anymore. We never would have killed him. We just wanted to hurt and humiliate him. He was weak and defeated; we just wanted to make things worse. We did it because we were afraid. We did just what the two Johns and Porky Bob did to Gary and me by taking us up to High-drive and for the same reasons. Always in this still wild land of the West—and, remember please, that every thing in this country that became the United States was always west; when the Pilgrims stepped onto Plymouth Rock and looked at the terrifying wilderness in front of them, they were looking west—we are all afraid, us strangers to the land, of the unknown creatures and things around us. It doesn't make any difference if *we* are the 7th Cavalry swooping down upon the women and children at Sand Creek, or, in sweet Custer-revenge, holding the final massacre at Wounded Knee; or, if *we* are my friends and I, tossing beer-cans into the truck-beds filled with wet-back labor just to know that they would hurt each other in fighting for the beer. It's the same story. The strong rape and pillage among the weak, while hiding themselves from the stronger; everybody hates the beaten and defeated because in the land of strangeness everybody was afraid. So, roll a drunk Indian because he was desperate and foolish enough to get drunk and collapse, homeless, in a dark alley. If you're a white boy with money fuck a black whore, a red whore, a yellow whore. They're not your girlfriends are they, fellas? You're not gonna take 'em home to Mama are you? Hell no, in my imagination, in your imagination, girlfriends sit at home with their Mamas, being good, nice and safe, waiting for their boyfriends to grow up and marry them. Holding tight to their cherries, letting the boyfriends feel their breasts now and again, maybe daring to squeeze an erection through a straining pair of jeans; while the boys go out to fight each other or strangers and fuck girls they pick up or, even, eat whores in the rooms of Wallace and Kellogg. Or, maybe, the girls are going out fucking strangers. At night, the world starts to howl; a wild babble of human voices, baying at the moon. Nobody hears, because everybody is too busy trying to listen to whatever it is that is shrieking inside of him or her. I wonder if Crazy Horse could sit still on the edge of a high cliff and look down at the Columbia River beneath him and chant in his head a song that would bring him into union with the river, the sky and the red-brown cliff he sat on? I wonder if he ever went to the Columbia River, if the wind would feel different to his face than it does to mine? I want it to. I want the world to be real, and if I can't experience it as such, then, at least, I want someone to sense its reality. When I was a little boy, I wanted that someone to be my grandfather. Walking with him in the woods made me believe in the reality of the touch and smell of the natural world. But then, I discovered him to be a dreamer like all the others. He set the eyes of his mind on the future. He wanted us to find the Northwest Passage. He really did. While his hands might be busy in the here and now of the natural moment, his mind danced in the unsubstantial air of the future. When I think about my doubleness—the "nice" person who can behave like a monster—I really know that there is a third who walks inside my mind. One part of me would deny Crazy Horse, another would try to kill him, but the third would want to sit beside him and evaporate into the world.

I wish I knew how to say that right. I wish I knew how to think it right. But, then, if I did, I would be there, not here in the wilderness of these walls of this cabin in the snow, listening to the howl of the winds and praying for the return of a dog. I know what's in my mind, but I can't say it right, even if I'm only talking to myself. It's not the booze and it's not the withdrawal. It's a jam-up. It all has to do with violence and with race and, because I lived in the goddamn East, with class. That's half of it. The other half is love—screaming, shrieking love that keeps stumbling over its tongue. I never wanted to destroy things or hurt people because of hate. Crazy as this sounds, it was because I didn't want to hate. My father hated and he gloried in his hate. Not me. I have always been afraid of people with different colored skins. When my mother told me that "niggers" would kill me if I called them by that word, I was stunned. I didn't want to be afraid of anyone; I was still a child in the world. After that I became cautious, fearful that I might be killed because I was different. I never liked the language of racism, particularly as I heard it in the rage of my father and, as I grew older and met blacks, Indians and Asians and became friends with them I would use the words of racism ironically with them, trying to tell them that I wasn't racist and yet, unconsciously, perhaps, making sure that they knew that I was aware of the difference between us and that, somewhere, I was afraid. I never went out to get "into trouble" by fighting or trying to pick up women with a person of another race; nor did I ever fight with one or try to pick one up. My black or

Asian or Indian friends never saw the violence that lived in my heart; and, as a consequence, they never knew the love. I treated them the way I would anyone who I felt held power over me, with a false deference and an attempt to present my "nice" side that bordered on fawning. I did want to marry Debra Paget, if she were truly an Indian, but to do so I would have to act like Jimmy Stewart. She would never have wanted me, and Cochise would never have accepted me as a son-in-law. Not the way I was. I wasn't brave enough, I wasn't tough enough to succeed in the world of my imagination, which, when you come right down to it, was my West. My West was—and is—both an arid desert and a rain forest. It is filled with mean people, venal people, brutal, sadistic monsters who like only to kill and maim; it is filled with gentle, caring people, people who touch the world and the creatures who live within it with love. In my imagination it is never kindness that reigns, no more than it is mindless brutality. It is always bravery. In *Broken Arrow*, Jimmy Stewart is kind and nice, but most of all he is brave. He goes alone into the Indian Camp. He is brave in the same way that Jeff Chandler, as Cochise, is brave. He is himself. Cochise is himself. Stewart's bravery is what earns him the love of Cochise's daughter. Stewart, Fonda and Gary Cooper flash across my mind in screen images of strong, smart, kind, brave men who deal with the world they live in honestly, with passion and with reason. When, in contrast, John Wayne's image appears to me, it is of a giant, one who wins because he is strongest; if he triumphs in a just cause, it seems almost accidental. He is heading from his very first movie image to the unknowable isolato that is Ethan in *The Searchers*. What scares me so much about the West that I live in is the idea I have that brute force triumphs. It isn't violence or rape or racism that frightens me. It's what lies beneath all three, in whatever combination that one finds them; it's the idea that because we cannot make sense out of our world, the strong attack and humiliate and destroy the weak. They are afraid that there is something even stronger—some terrifying monster of the wilderness—that they have never seen but that they know would kill them if it could. There's desperation here, a desperation that is as simple as fear. If we touch the flame we will burn. Why did—do—the whites hate the Indians? Because they were savages? No, we called them that because we, from the very first contact, knew there was a difference, and we called them savages because we wanted them to be potential murderers, we wanted to fear them, because then we could hate and destroy them. If we were afraid of them, as we were afraid of the wolf and the bear, then we could seize power over them. If we were full of terrified hatred, and they were merely curious, we could destroy them.

* * *

This is simple-minded bullshit.

* * *

I know that.

* * *

But my mind is so simple now, so twisted by fear and sadness and loss, that I must try to get back to first things. I hear a howl under the wind now. Is it the dog? Is it Crazy Horse? Is it a wolf wandered down out of the snow, drawn by the lights of the cabin? Am I afraid? Don't you see, I must get beneath my fear. If I start afraid I will want to destroy, to rape, to hurt and end up, hopeless as that doomed monkey or Jack-Time, huddled in a corner of the cabin trying to jack-off, without desire, without potency—just a pathetic, futile exercise in self-destruction.

No. No. Not now, not yet. I turn the lights out in the cabin. The fire still glows, but now it is dark all around me. I open the door cautiously. No dog. I step outside. It is not snowing. The air is almost too cold for snow. There is a clear, bright half-moon above the pines. The wind is sharp and brittle off the lake. I hear the howl again. It is a wolf. I suck in the cold air and answer it, sending a cry into the night. Then silence. I stand there in the winter dark, no coat, no hat, no gloves. The wind feels good. I pick up a handful of snow and rub it in my hair, on my face. Oh, God! I would like to pull off my clothes and run naked into the wind, down onto the ice of the lake, run until I plunged, gasping, off the edge of the ice and into the deep, dark waters of the lake. Of course, I won't.

I wish I could stop repeating myself. Over and over, I say the same things over and over in my head. The things that I did, the things that happened, o.k.—there each memory, each story is a thing unto itself. But, whenever I look for a reason, I fall back on goddamn history, on goddamn movies, or just plain goddamn fear. Goddamn fear of what? I keep saying other people or strange circumstances, but is that all there is to it? Am I—are we all—just so goddamn afraid of being alone, of being unloved (God! I want to spit when I say that word!) that it ruins our lives? Weak, fucking vessels. This is where I get so tired. I walk down this pitch-black alley, with all the noises of the universe around me, and then I turn on my flashlight at the dead-end and see my own face giant on a brick wall? Oh, Jesus, no! Not that one. You see, I don't want to just think about myself. I don't want to believe that my mother and father are dead, that my wife shit on my weakness and threw me out of my life. If I think about love—whatever the hell that means—or the lack of love, I *will* end up in that blind alley of poor-me and I *will* see my own face on the wall and I *will* cry senseless tears of self pity. I won't learn anything. Why do I wish my parents were still alive? Is it because their lives were special and precious to me? No, it is because they knew me. No matter how separated we were—how much they left me alone when I was a child, how far I ran from them when I was an adult—they meant that I had a history; and, like any educated American white man in the 20th Century, history is important to me. History brings me civilization and separates me from the beasts. People say that Indians believe in spirits, that they believe that the spirits of the dead remain in the land they lived in. This kind of history is anti-history. It means that everything is in every moment of time, that living and dead, past and present are with us with each breath we take. My mother believed in a heaven that was just like an eternal family reunion; everyone together, laughing and smiling through eternity. I don't believe in an after-life, family reunion or no. But, I'll tell you what I wish I could believe. I'd like to believe that if I went down to the lakeshore now, and chipped through the ice, cupped my hand and took a drink of the cold lake water, that I would be drinking my mother, my father, my grandfather and all the other people who have gone before me. Or, with each full, deep breath I take of the lake and mountain air that I am breathing all of them into my lungs. Wouldn't that be wonderful! You see, I don't really believe in history at all. History means that everything ends up in me, and that can't be the way the world is. There has to be a world that I don't know, but it can't be a world, like the Christian Heaven my mother believed in, that other people imagined. It has to be real. I don't want to hurt people anymore. I don't want to hurt myself. I don't want to drink. I don't want to die. Yet I will probably do all four; certainly the last. I want to find a place of stillness where I can live. I want to find a place in my mind or my heart where nothing will shock me; so that, even if monsters appear to me walking out of the forest or down a city street, I can recognize them and yet walk on, feeling no need to strike out or, even, to protect myself. If I stand still now and close my eyes to the light of the stars and the moon, I can still feel the snow on my hands and my face but, even more, I can feel the wind on my skin, I can feel it in my ears—there is a high, fine roar to it. I feel the sound. I smell the sound, too, and I smell the lake and the pines and the firs mixed together in the wind. The smell bites at the back of my throat, as though I have been chewing the living needles from the trees. Now, I open my eyes and the night stars blind me. They seem so close and a part of the wind that roars around me. And the moon too; and the dark, blue-black reaches of the cloudless sky. All carried in the wind that seems to rush through my body. I lift my legs up and pull off my shoes and socks, I drop my pants and underwear and step out of them, I pull my shirt over my head. I feel as though

I am exploding into the world around me. I feel one with the wind. Not cold. Every part of my body feels as though electricity were running through it. I start to pant. How long can I continue . . . how long can I stand naked in the winter night? Shall I?

*   *   *

No. Not yet. I put my clothes on again and return to the cabin. The lake will wait for me. I'm dizzy now. The wind and the sounds of the night have left me buzzing and humming all over. I must just be quiet. Not think. Listen to the sound of my body and the sound of the wind. A wolf cries and I answer. There is so much sound in the world if I can quiet my thoughts enough to listen to it. I feel as though I were a little boy again. When we lived near the edge of the swamp, I loved to "play hide." There were trees behind our house; a grove of old pines ran from the house to the dirt road at the edge of the swamp. When I was six, my friend from down the street, Jim, and I built a tree house in a tree that we felt was in the wilderness. It was probably no more than a few hundred yards from our house, but when we climbed up we couldn't see the house. We saw nothing but forest, and, because we lived at what was then the edge of the town, we heard no cars, only the sounds of the forest. Our tree house was no more than a platform of two-by-fours that ran over three level branches. There was just room for two small boys. We nailed wood blocks into the trunk of the tree for a makeshift ladder. This was my favorite place to "play hide." Early in the morning, I would tell my mother that I was going down to Jim's house to play, and, instead, I would go out into the woods and climb up into the tree house. There I would sit, with my back against the tree-trunk, and listen to the forest talk. There, just as I felt now, standing naked in the winter lake night, I would feel the sound of the wind in the trees, feel the sound of the birds, feel the sound of the insects buzzing around me. It seemed as though I could sit forever, as though I had been taken out of time. I was able not to think. What a blessing!

In the "real" world, of course, my time in paradise was limited to a few days. Jim came to my house one morning and brought my worried mother to the tree house. The secret ended. I still went to the tree house by myself, but the magic was gone. I knew that my mother could arrive at any moment. I found myself listening for her noise in the midst of the forest sounds. Jim and his younger brother, David, and I began to play war games in the woods. David, even though he complained and sometimes even cried about it, had to play the Jap because he was the youngest. Jim and I were brave, honest Americans. We pretended to be working on different projects, like digging foxholes, while David sneaked up on us, crawling through the woods, trying to be quiet. At just the last moment, Jim and I would stop digging and turn on David's creeping figure and yell, "Die Jap! Die Jap! This is for all of our buddies you've killed! Die! Die!" while pointing our finger-guns at him and firing. He never had a chance. Then we started to explore the swamp, and to climb Big Rock, and to ask Bunny, who lived next door to Jim and David, if we could look inside her underpants. As far as I know, the tree house stayed up until they cut down the forest for a housing development. By then, none of us lived in that neighborhood anymore.

You see how easily it happens? I'm still naked. But I'm now standing in the cabin, out of the wind, and suddenly I stop feeling and my mind leaps into the past. I can't stop at the tree house and just sit there for a while without thinking. And thinking puts me back into history; and from the smell of the forest, I'm suddenly remembering how embarrassed I was after I asked Bunny to look inside her underpants, when, less than a week later, sitting on top of Big Rock, she took them right off when Dean—who was two years older—asked her to and she turned her back on me and showed herself to Dean. Why do I need to remember that? Would I like to see in Bunny's underpants now? Would I like to fuck Ida Greycloud? Would I like to say, "Die, Jap!" to Joe Takashita as he mowed a rich man's lawn? Who the fuck knows? Not me. That's just it, I don't know. People who claim to know live direct lives. They are born, they learn how to do a variety of things over a number of years and then they die. No ripple is made. No scream is heard. But they claim to know. A white boy who claimed to know would not fuck Ida Greycloud, would not yell, "Die, Jap!" at Joe Takashita. His parents wouldn't let him; and, when he became his parents, he wouldn't let his son misbehave. But, they only claim to know, and that "knowledge" makes them cautious with their lives and their experiences. They walk slowly and deliberately from place to place, being careful not to bump into anyone else. I have never been able to do that.

My high-school friend Ross's dad "claimed to

know," and Ross hero-worshipped him. When I first met him, at 15, he was very precise around us. He set himself as an expert and he would tell us exactly how we should behave; what we should say; what we should think about things. I thought he was like a minister or a very prissy teacher. I figure that Ross must have had some doubts all along, because one day he searched his dad's study when both of his parents were out. He never told me what he was looking for, but he sure told me what he found. In a bottom drawer of his dad's desk he found a dozen photographs. They were real pictures of live people fucking and sucking each other; even one picture of a guy wearing only his socks shooting a big gob of jism all over a woman's breasts. We'd never seen anything like them before. He also found a towel, with the name Rosso sewn into the fabric. It was stiff and crinkled and it stank of cum. It was his dad's jack-rag. Ross figured that his dad must warm it up somehow to make it soft and then sit behind his desk and look at the pictures and jack off and send his load into the rag. It was an incredible thing to find. We barely knew what we were doing when we jacked-off, and Ross figured that his dad had been using the towel as a jack-rag for years. It sure smelled like it. Ross and I stopped hanging out together shortly after that time, but a couple of years later he told me a story that served, at least in my mind, as a fitting conclusion to his discovery. Ross had found himself a high-school girlfriend who would go all the way with him. Not many of us could say the same, so Ross boasted about it a lot. His girl lived in an apartment with her divorced mother. One afternoon, according to Ross, when he and his girl were alone in the apartment and about to do it, Ross opened a bedroom closet and there, on a hanger, was a pair of his father's pajamas, with Rosso embroidered on the pocket. Ross put them on and had his girl take a Polaroid of him wearing them. He mailed it to his dad at his office. After that, Ross said, he and his father would double date with the girl and her mother. Ross thought it was a terrific joke on his mother, who he described, quoting his dad, as a "frigid bitch." Ross's dad had a shiny veneer. He claimed to lead a straight, direct, moral life. He was a worthless bastard.

Maybe everybody is. Maybe nobody is "straight" in the world. Maybe everybody wishes that he or she could have seen inside his or her own particular version of Bunny's underpants. Maybe most people actually fuck their own versions of Ida Greycloud and nobody ever knows. Maybe everybody has pajamas with Rosso embroidered on them hanging in their minds. Little secret places where we can hide the world's jack-rags. Ross's dad was a lawyer. My father respected him. Ross's dad did legal work for the people who owned downtown Spokane. When they decided to change the city for a World's Fair and "cleaned" it up, built the skywalks, polished the sidewalks, and threw all the poor whites and Indians out of town, Ross's dad made sure it was all legal. I think of him now jacking-off behind his desk while he was helping to ruin the city, maybe having a fantasy about fucking a beautiful Indian girl. When I see Spokane now, with its empty downtown streets and its packed, sprawling suburban malls, I see dead Indians, and bits and pieces of deadbeat, drunk

white beggars, hacked to death, drawn and quartered by the big machines that made the city pretty enough for a year of tourists. The ancestors of the men who killed Spokane had run away from the towns of Ohio and Illinois to find some room to live in, I imagine they thought of growth, that they had some version of the goofy Men-to-Match-My-Mountains western catchphrase. I don't think they wanted to replicate

Peoria or Cherry Grove. They wanted to kill Indians, since the history of the Republic had taught them that the Indians wouldn't be domesticated; like the wolves or the bears, they had to be cleared from the land that the white men wanted. But it's hard for me to believe that they wanted only to destroy, to turn the whole goddamn land into the consumer's parking lot it is becoming. That couldn't have been their vision. In the main, they were scared little losers, not demons. But I don't know about men like Ross's dad. I don't think that he gave a shit about anything except making money and gratifying his petty little lusts. It makes me sick to think about him, and, goddamnit, now I've got fathers in my mind. Mine, Ross's and John's. John's father was a dentist—ah, these professional men—and he used to beat John regularly, even through high school. He would wake him in the middle of the night, for no apparent reason, beat him and make get up and shovel coal for their furnace. He thought I was a "pussy-chaser"—god knows I was at sixteen, but with pathetically little success—and thought it was funny to ridicule me: "That's not love-light in your eyes, son, that's tail-light;" or, "You're one kid who's on the road to early fatherhood," he'd say, winking meanly. All he wanted was to make us feel weak, dumb and silly. He didn't like the fact that we were actors, and he really didn't like the affection his wife showed towards us. I'm sure he never knew that we used their cabin at Twin Lakes, or, this for sure, that his wife gave me a key to the cabin. And, of course, there's my father, who never really leaves my mind. My mother used to tell me how much he loved me when I was a baby. I don't think she ever knew that her telling me that only made me wonder what ever happened to that love. That's the kind of wondering I don't want to do.

* * *

I'm starting to feel the cold now, leaning here with my hands against the wall, staring out the window into the blank night of the trees with the glints of starlight on them. It's time to either get dressed again or go back outside and walk into the wind. Now or later? I'll opt for later and get dressed. I think I'm clear of the booze now. I finished off the dregs of the vodka and—fingers crossed—I think I'm managing the withdrawal. If I can focus on real memories and not let my mind chase after fantasies, I may be able to see clearly. I miss that dog.

* * *

My uncle Robert owned a linoleum store in Ballard. He also owned a small farm in Edmonds, which he sold to buy a big farm in Kittitas. I loved him and I loved his life. I thought he was a good and honest man. When my mother died, I flew to Seattle from the East Coast for the funeral. I was addicted to Valium and a serious, bad drunk. I was hiding it all. I had shoulder-length hair and a beard—I probably looked a little like some of the pictures of Custer, not at all like Castro or Che Guevara, who I wanted to look like—and Robert didn't like the beard. He had joined the John Birch Society as his reaction to the Viet Nam War, and, when he saw me after the funeral, he called me a "god-damn Commie," and turned his back on me. He mellowed in later years, but I never really did. I'll always remember the look he gave me. So much for good and honest men. When my first wife cut me adrift because I was an alcoholic and in a coma with liver failure, she told my children that I had died. She later told me that it would have been best for everyone if I had died. The logic of how that would have been best for me eludes me still. When I came out of the hospital, my aunt, Robert's wife, told me that God's plan was one man for one woman and that, because I was a drunk, I was sentenced to a life alone.

I have to back off here. This shit is too real. I'm getting mad and I don't know how to deal with that anger. I'm sober, and if I think too much about rejection or the crazy personal things people say and do, I won't be able to keep focused. I don't want to fall into some mire of sentimental self-pity. I am not "poor me." I have chosen to be here, where and who I am.

* * *

When my grandfather traded his Montana homestead for a donut recipe, he also got a tiny piece of land in the woods east of Everett, in a place called Cathcart, which was almost in the foothills of the Cascades. There was a broken-down one-room shack on the property, but no out-house. Like bears, if people needed to shit or piss, they did it in the woods. It was about a half-mile walk from a dirt road to the house, and you had to carry in any food or water you might need. At the age of five, it seemed as wild as any thing in the world could be. I only went there twice. After the second time, my mother flatly refused to go to Cathcart. The first time we went there, I walked into the woods with my grandfather and watched him gather fallen tree-limbs for firewood. The woods were beautiful to me. The smell of the cedar trees was intoxicating, and the way the light filtered through the tall trees made it look like some twilight fairy kingdom. I felt like Peter Pan. I had learned how to read, and had read Peter Pan until the story became part of my dreams and my fantasies. When we went back to Seattle that night, I felt as though I had been touched by magic. I could hardly wait to go to Cathcart again. We went back a week later and this time I did not go into the woods with my grandfather. When all the adults were busy talking and trying to clean in and around the cabin, I went into the woods by myself. There were no cousins with us, just my grandparents, my mother and two of her sisters, so, when I saw the chance, I was on my own. I dreamed up Tinkerbell, and followed my dream image of her into the cedar forest. It was wet in the forest. Not raining,

but wet with a damp mist brightened by the sunlight filtered through the trees. The air filled my nostrils with all the smells of the woods. Cedar. Fir. And, as I remember, the faint scents of the flowers growing among the ferns on the fallen trees. Oh, how I wanted to fly like Peter Pan! I wanted to go high up, into the tallest cedars and fly or leap from branch to branch, tree to tree. It was like a wonderful dream and I walked deeper into the forest, climbing over nurse-logs and discovering secret hiding places in the hollowed trunks of towering dead trees. I was far from the Cathcart cabin and out of the time in which my mother, aunts and grandparents lived. In my child's mind I felt in the time eternal of the forest of the real world. Then I saw her. First, just a fleeting glance of cloth moving behind a tree-trunk, then a small figure darted into a heavy growth of ferns. What was it? Was it the spirit of the forest? I ran after the figure. Just as I reached the ferns, she stood up, no more than a few feet from me. It was a girl. Maybe my own age. Maybe Wendy? She smiled at me and held out her hand. I reached out and took it. Her fingers were cool like the ferns. We did not speak. She led me into the ferns. It was thick and green; a fern forest. They were higher than our heads, wet and dense with the dew and water from the air. I watched the droplets of water seem to bounce off her hair and shoulders. On the other side of the ferns was a giant rock. Not a hill, but a huge boulder. It had a hole in it. She crawled into the hole, still holding my hand and pulling me after her. The hole was not a tunnel; it was a door. I could stand up inside the rock. She smiled at me again and gestured around her with her arm. It was a real, little room. There were chairs and a small table made out of pieces of cedar and tied together with vines. There was a small bed and a little circle in the center of the room where a fire was built. It was perfect. It was her size. It was my size. She pointed at one of the chairs for me to sit. I did. We still did not talk. Then she got a bowl of berries from a ledge on the wall, put it on the table and sat down on the other chair. She handed me a berry. I ate it. She ate one and smiled again. We sat and ate berries and smiled at each other. When the berries were gone, she stood up and walked over and kissed me. Then she took my hand again and led me out of the rock, through the ferns, and, pointing in the direction in which I was to go, went back into the ferns again. I pushed into the ferns, but I couldn't find her. I went through the ferns and out the other side, and there was no rock. Just the forest all around me. She had disappeared. And so had her rock-home.

I went back through the ferns again and followed the direction she had pointed out to me as well as I could. I finally got back to Cathcart. I told my mother what had happened to me, and that was when she decided that we wouldn't go back to Cathcart again.

I don't know why I remembered that now. I never think about that particular incident. I think that's because everyone thought that I had made it up. My imagination was too vivid—that kind of attitude from my adult relatives—it was dangerous for me to be in the woods, particularly in wild forest, without adult supervision. In other words, I was a crazy little kid. They never thought, not even for a second, that my story could have been true, that it actually happened. But I saw the little girl. I touched her hand. I smelled her. She kissed me and I felt her lips on mine. If they had looked, they would have found berry stains on my fingertips when I came back to the cabin. But, of course, they would have said that I picked wild blackberries in the woods. They didn't know. Why couldn't she have been real? If, seven or eight years later, I could walk into the woods and run into a giant pervert in bib-overalls, why couldn't I be kissed by a little, quiet girl in a room in a cave in a rock?

Maybe I wanted to stay there. There can be a magic in reality. I think that's what Crazy Horse knows. I think that's why I want to believe in him. Believe that he is alive, in whatever form he might have taken; whatever shape he might have shifted into. I know that the little girl kissed me, whether she was real in any way that my mother might have understood. When I think of that moment, I can taste the sweet berry of her lips.

* * *

You see, Doctor, I don't need you anymore. I don't need to make believe that I'm talking to you. You can't help me answer any questions because I don't have any more. I'm tired, and I just want to think about things. Quietly. Real things. Like the little girl's kiss, like the taste of the whore, like the smell of the wino after he'd pissed his pants, like the way the dead Indian's face looked under the light in Trent Alley, like the way Topper's breath smelled the first time I kissed her, like the shape of that stupid cowboy's head in the palm of my hand as I smashed his face again and again into his car bumper in the back parking lot of the State-Line Gardens. Things like that. Those aren't questions. There are no moral dilemmas anywhere. It's just the real world. That's all it's ever been.

Rip-saw Joe and Hand-axe Pete were just a couple of losers from Pennsylvania who gave themselves nicknames and left their families and got on a train to what was going to be Glacier Park. They acted like lumberjacks and carpenters and one of them wore women's underwear. End of story. End of fucking story. My father's father got on a boat in Sweden and ended up crossing the whole goddamn North America to sit at night guarding a Seattle reservoir. His son went to High School, and then sold life insurance to Indians. Crazy! These are Western Stories? They may be if they are all we have. There may be beautiful little girls wandering in our woods. There may be sick fuckers wandering in our woods. There may be the remnants of Indians wandering in our woods. We may find them all if we, too, wander. Wandering is our Western Story. We don't want to own a general store or a saloon; we don't want to preach or teach. We don't want to sell insurance. We don't want to have insurance. We want to wander through our beautiful, goddamn woods. We want to kiss our forests, hold our mountains in our arms, and take our rivers in our mouths. I know I, and I say we because I know I am not alone. I am not Jack-Time Elias. This is not my fantasy. It is my life I am telling. But it belongs to others as well. Anyone who has ever walked alone in the Western forests, or on the hard surface of the Western deserts, or in the Western meadows, or on the streets of a Western town, knows precisely what I mean when I say that under all the hard facts that we can draw out of our time-lines in our life-times, the world is screaming at us to see it before it is too late. But we don't listen, or we can't hear it; or, saddest of all, we don't believe it. The voice of the world is not the idle, sentimental or malicious chatter of humankind. Its scream is a whisper that lies between the world as it is and what we try to do with it. I wish, sometimes, that I could believe in pure spirit and in its ability to manifest itself in visible form. I wish, for instance, that just as people raised the scoops and blades of their enormous machines to destroy the Great Swamp that I loved so much, that the spirit of the earth could have raised its roaring bulk out of the swamp and, shouting "No!" would have smashed the machines and sent the people running back to their petty, paved world. Right now I wish that the dog hadn't left me alone. I wish he had revealed himself to me as Crazy Horse. Then I would have met the spirit of the earth.

Or if I could have become Peter Pan and the little girl in the woods had been Wendy and I could have lived inside the rock forever. If I were to let go now, what would I see, what dreamscape, what vision? I sit down on the floor. I cross my legs. A lotus position. I close my eyes and breath deeply. The door to the cabin opens and a beautiful woman stands there. Her long hair is swirling about in the wind from the winter night. It changes color from an almost white blond to the deepest black and back again. Her eyes are the bright blue of the dog. Crazy Horse's eyes. She wears just a long blanket over her shoulders. She smiles at me and then she lets the blanket fall to the floor. Oh my! She is still smiling as she walks towards me. When she reaches me she kneels and kisses me. Then she puts her arms around me and I respond by holding her. She smells so purely of nature that I am a child again, drunk on the scent of the cedars and the wet mosses and grasses. She takes me into her and holds me there for what seems like an exquisite eternity. Then she kisses me again. And smiles. And, she is gone.

And now, do I dare to open my eyes? Is that what I have wanted? To have a union like that? Is that what it is like to be at home in the world? I don't know. I only know that with my eyes open and the cabin the reality around me that I can still smell her and the pure natural scent that enveloped her. I don't know what that means, about my sanity or anything else. This is something different. I want the purity of the vision to stay with me, but if I try too hard, I see something else entirely. I am five, or six, or, maybe even seven. I am out at Manito Golf Club for dinner with my parents. I can't go into the bar where they sit, my father drinking, my mother playing the slots, for an hour or so before we eat. I wait in the big lobby room, with leather furniture and a fireplace. I look at copies of *Esquire* magazine. When I have to go to the bathroom I walk by the cloakroom, and as I do so I glance inside. There is my father embracing some woman. I can't see her face because they are kissing and her back is turned to me. But I see his hands squeezing her buttocks. Try to get that image out of your mind. Who was she? I don't know. I don't care. She was somebody's wife. Somebody's nice respectable drunken wife. And, as my father would say, Mina was a whore. Not the bitch in the cloakroom, stinking of gin, smearing her fucking lipstick all over my father's mouth. She's a respectable woman. She's got a good middle-class marriage, maybe kids at home, maybe kids in my school, maybe she fucks Ross's dad.

There's too big a distance between what I want to be real and what is. If I want to walk barefoot in the woods feeling the path with my natural skin, what I do is drive 75 miles an hour the wrong way on a one-way street, ticking my rear-vision mirror on the mirrors on the driver's sides of the parked cars. I call it precisioning. I only ever did it when I was drunk and young enough to be crazy brave. If I want a pure smile of love and connection, what I talk myself into seeing is my father grinding away in the Manito cloakroom, or what I hear is my ex-wife telling me that she could never use enough mouthwash to get rid of the hideous memory of the taste of sucking my cock.

* * *

A graduate student once told me that I had been a Plains Indian in my previous life. He was a disciple of Sri Chinmoy until he started keeping the money he collected to finance his own ashram. He was a con-man, no doubt about it, so crafty and devious that he convinced everybody that he was harmless and crazy; he got his own teen-age disciples to run away from home and work for him, the young girls he used for sex. He claimed that he was an incarnation of Vishnu. I used to laugh at him; sober, I found him despicable. Yet, all things thought through, I wished—and still wish—that what he said about my having been an Indian were true. It would give me something that I could look at as substance, instead of seeing myself as a little white boy grown old, unhappy and whiny because the world isn't the way he would like it to be. No, if Goofy Fred would have been true and honest and right about just that one thing, then in my Indian wisdom I could forgive him all his cruelties and stupidities. But, I'm afraid that it was bullshit just like all the other things he said. He only told me that, as he read my palm, because he knew I would like to hear it and saying it might help him in some way. A few years after Sri let him go and after he had his own ashram, although as a "true American" (as he referred to himself) it was in Silicon Valley and his followers were computer programmers fired up with Jolt Cola, well, after that and making a fortune and starting a Zen Rock band, he fell off a dock out in front of his Oldfield, N.Y. mansion and gave up his karma to Long Island Sound. So, in the end nothing helped him and it really makes no difference if, in particularly strange moments, I choose to believe him and feel myself, bareback, riding down the wind with Crazy Horse at my side; or, if I watch myself, naked under my shirt, Ghost Dancing while Sitting Bull watches from inside the Sacred Circle. At those times, believing Fred, I can taste the air I breathe; I roar in the dust clouds of the high desert land in which I was born and know that it is the same as the air I breathed a century ago at Wounded Knee. And I can feel myself, walking with the sure step of Leschi, in the deep rain forests of the Western Cascades. I have just been there, and my head races with the images. Has it always been this way? When I was a little boy, in the Great Swamp or walking in the woods at Cathcart, were my eyes closed? Was I breathing and hearing and touching the world? And when I walked the streets of Spokane, were my eyes open? And was all I saw destruction? Is that why I taste the blood in my mouth, and walk, arms open for an embrace, into violence and danger? If I could touch the world, why would I want to fight with it? Oh, My God! Why did Gary and I steal the hat from the dead Indian's head in Trent Alley?

There is something in that action that is like a knife thrust to the heart. It wasn't so bad that we went to downtown Spokane at night. It wasn't so bad that we chose to walk into Trent Alley. It scared us. We knew that Indians would be there. The Indian taverns faced on to Main and had their back doors on Trent Alley. Indians would cross Trent from the railroad tracks, yards and train station and often enter the Mint or the Buck and Doe from the alley between Trent and Main. At the age of fourteen, we felt as though we were entering an Indian Camp, our heads were dancing with danger. From the time when I was a small boy downtown shopping with my mother, I remember the Indian taverns. I could catch furtive

glances into the big plate glass windows on the front of them as my mother would race past, dragging me behind her. It was exotic to me as a child when my mother would whisper: "That's an Indian bar." As I grew older the forbidden, exotic Indian bar became an object of real curiosity to me. If I close my eyes now, I can smell the rancid smell of cigarettes and sweet wine that would come from the doorway if the door opened when I was walking by it. I can see the back bar lined with bottles of muscatel, tokay and port. Cheap, fortified wines that the Indians drank since it was so hard for them to buy liquor at the State Stores. The Mint and the Buck and Doe were right next to each other and almost identical. Indians leaned against the lamppost out in front of the Mint and sat on the sidewalk in front of the windows of the taverns. They always seemed to be laughing and talking and when you walked by them they would make remarks and then laugh among themselves. The alley behind the taverns was for sleeping, and any time of day or night a wanderer would find Indians curled up in the stairwells or behind the trashcans. I know, I know, I know—they were drinking themselves to death. I suppose I knew it then, but, now, having tried it myself, talking about *what* they were doing to themselves with the cheap wine seems so obvious as to be almost unimportant. Yes, it was a horror show, but it was what they had. Denied access to the white man's world, jobs or society, they were corralled into a tiny section of downtown Spokane land: the Great Northern Station, the land between the station and Trent; about half a block of both Trent and Main and the alley that lay between the two streets. That was the Reservation for the Urban Indians, that small band that left the Reservation and direct United States government control for the possibility of gandy dancing or janitorial work or, simply, panhandling for money. I think that as kids we felt that there was something unusual in the grouping of the Indians; I know we saw the mixture of fear and contempt among our elders. They acted afraid to touch the Indians, as though their poverty could be contagious. I was fascinated by the Indians and whenever I was downtown with my mother—and later on from about the age of ten, when I could go downtown by myself—I would try to hide myself in the people walking on the sidewalks across the street from the taverns and watch the Indians. Sometimes the laughter in the group would break and arguments would erupt, sometimes fights and two Indians would swing wildly at each other, grapple and fall to the sidewalk and then roll off the sidewalk into the street between parked cars. No police ever broke up these fights. In fact, I don't think I ever saw a policeman on that half-block of Main Street. No whites, not even transients, ever went into the Mint or the Buck and Doe, and the Indians never crossed Main Street. Looking back with the eyes I have now, I can see that what existed in Spokane was a sort of Treaty. Having taken away everything that the Indians were used to having access to and calling it private property, the Whites had ceded a tiny portion of urban land to the Indians to enable them to destroy themselves privately. So long as they self-destructed on the pocket of land provided for them, they would be left alone. Until, that is, the White Fathers of Spokane decided that they needed to clean up their city for tourists. Then they threw the Indians out of town, paved over the generations of vomit and blood in Trent Alley and replaced the Mint and the Buck and Doe with fancy restaurants and wine bars. The Reservation became Riverfront Park and no more Indians accidentally drowned in the Spokane River.

That's now, and it represents Spokane's attempt to become a Northwest version of Orlando. A pure fantasy, with an ancient merry-go-round at its center, doomed to failure from the start; not even the whores are left from Spokane's World's Fair season.

But I don't care about now, or some goddamn future vision. I want to go back to Gary and me in Trent Alley standing over the body of the dead Indian. What did it mean when Gary grabbed the hat off his head and handed it to me and I stuffed it in my pocket? Counting coup on a corpse? We were so excited and frightened that we didn't think at all about what we were doing. We hadn't really gone down to the Alley hoping to roll a drunk Indian. It felt like—because we didn't think at all—we were white raiders sneaking into an Indian camp. We had talked about rolling a drunk Indian, but that was just talk. We were fourteen and we were old enough to be really scared, and we knew enough about Indians to know that they might really kill us and feel justified in doing it. So, when I spoke to the dead Indian it took great courage; the same when Gary lifted his hat. But, when we saw that he was dead and took the hat and ran, that was not courage, it was bald fear. We violated him for no reason, save that we were scared and stupid kids. We did not understand or even know respect. We were afraid for ourselves. We did not recognize the fact that we were with a dead man. He wasn't real to us as a person. He had had no life for us. In our eyes he merited no more respect than if he had been a mannequin lying in the trash behind a department store. We ran because we were afraid we would be blamed for littering as much as for killing. For us, that which had never really had value alive could have none dead. His death wasn't real. Our fantasy of sneaking into the Indian Camp was. So, I can't hand myself that shit that we *violated* something sacred, that we committed some eternal moral crime that has haunted our lives ever since. We didn't break the hoop or destroy the circle. We didn't dishonor the dead. Just like everybody in our wretched, goddamn West, we didn't recognize the living. There was never any danger among the Indian habitués of Trent and Main and Trent Alley. If an Indian were to hurt a White in 20th Century Spokane, it would be thought of as a mad and rabid dog attack—just somebody's pet gone berserk and then put to sleep. That would be the punishment. Put to sleep. Indians weren't real to us. But since they weren't, what was? Wolves? Bear? Deer? Owls? My dad's Chrysler?

What should have happened when we lifted that hat and looked at those dead Indian eyes? Well, wouldn't it have been nice if we could have borrowed a technique from the movies and stared deep into the eyes and then dived down in and back in time to some sort of mythic tribal past? A world all green and brown. No concrete. No sidewalks, streets, buildings, cars. Animals and birds and flowers and trees. Sweet smells and sounds. Beautiful, barely clothed Indians. Wouldn't that have been nice? But, what if we'd looked deep into those dead eyes and seen a massacre. What if George Wright would have been there slaughtering horses and any people who didn't get away fast enough? That would not have been so nice. That old western feeling, the taste of blood when one looks at the roses. As the song says: "You can't have one without the other." No. We wouldn't have seen anything had we stopped to look into his eyes. Our nostrils would have been filled with the mixed stench of cheap wine, urine and shit from a corpse, and that would have been the sum of it. Seen nothing, done nothing. A couple of teen-agers riding a late night No. 6 bus up Monroe. One of them has a stinking old hat stuffed in his pocket. They're talking about something in hushes and laughing.

It's all the years at Manito Presbyterian Sunday School that makes me want to wish that I would have done something differently that night, or, at least felt something differently. Too much Jesus at too early an age; the missionary child has a terrible time losing his faith. I know a lot of white westerners who have "discovered" what they believe is Indian—although they would call it Native American—spirituality. Sometimes I think that I wish I could convince myself—delude myself—into believing that there really was such a thing as an Indian cosmology and that I could become a convert, shaking off the last remnants of my mother's teachings and forget how it felt to move the little Jesus figure over to watch the sheep on the felt board that stood on an easel in the Sunday school room of the church. But I can't do it. I can't believe in anything beyond my senses. I can say: "Everything that lives is sacred; everything that is sacred lives." I can believe that, but I have never really acted as though I do. I love the idea behind Ghost Dancing. All the whites on the continent would be destroyed, and all the dead Indians would come back and all the buffalo and the other animals. It is a wonderful belief for a doomed race of people. If I could believe in anything, it would be that, save, I would add that the whites could live and dead whites could come back if they would be able to respect life. So goddamn simple. I don't like death. I am more than willing to believe that everything natural lives—even stones and dust—I just don't want it to die. I didn't want my grandfather to die, or my parents, or Crazy Horse, or Sitting Bull, or, even, Bing Crosby. But they all did. Maybe. Or, maybe, Crazy Horse can change shapes and, right now he is running somewhere outside this cabin in the snow in the shape of a feral dog with beautiful eyes like my Aunt Mina; and, if he can do that, maybe they all could. But I don't know about any of that. I don't even know enough to think about it. I know that it was bad to kick my friend Doug in the balls outside the whorehouse in Iron City, but it was bad of him to say what he did. I know that it was bad to want to kill Neil at the initiation on Moran Prairie, but Neil could well have killed the initiates if I hadn't stopped him.

It was bad of the man with the horse-cock to give me dirty comic books to touch his hard-on in the men's room of the Eagles. That I know was bad. Real bad. It confused the hell out of me. One of the things that we did—I mean we white westerners—and do is hurt people for sport. I don't know if the Indians did this, when the tribes were intact, or not. Tossing beers into the back bed of the truck carrying wetback laborers is an example of what I mean. I did it for a laugh. We thought it was funny to watch the wetbacks tumble around and fight each other over warm beers. They weren't real to us. If they'd been real we never would have thought of them simply as wetbacks. Or, take Joe Takashita as an example. That poor bastard was in a concentration camp during the Second World War. We didn't know shit about him. We didn't care. To us he had no life before the war, during the war, or after it. He was just a little yellow man with a funny name that gave us an excuse—in our grade school brains—to yell, "Shit!" in the neighborhood. We could talk dirty and laugh and the only thing that stupid ass-hole Takashita could do was shake his rake at us. That's the way we saw it anyway. Wetbacks and Japs and Indians. Girls who were sluts and whores. Guys who were queers. Cripples. Old people. Drunks. Bums. The west was full of wonders for us nightriders and towntamers to behold and to conquer. And we did. If I could have respected my father and not called him "shitty-shorts" to my friends, we might have taken "Salsbury's the shits!" as our rallying cry. As it was, in high school we called ourselves the Blackcocks, after the "Blackhawk" comic book, and our cry was: "Cock-aaa!" Yeah. Sure. "Cock-aaa!" And we would drive off into the night in my father's old Chrysler, or the broken-down Nash Ambassador I inherited from my brother, or Fred's mother's Volvo—Ha! Ha! Ha! We're going to ride in Fred's mother's Vulva!—marauders with beer-cans as weapons; tail-gating slow-driving citizens, and then roaring past them with streams of obscenities; stopping to bend street signs over, or write "fuck you" on bus-stop benches; pulling into driveways and honking and flashing our lights until the people came out of the houses and we could give them the finger and yell "fuck you" right at them. Looking for trouble just so we could run a sortie and turn and escape capture or punishment. On the move, we thought of ourselves as Indians on war-ponies, darting into enemy camps, counting some sort of coup and racing out again. Usually we just went out to cause small trouble, insult people, damage public property. Once, when a group of us were at a cabin at Loon Lake, somebody said that whoever had the cabin next to us sure had a shitty car. We waited until the couple who owned the car were down at the beach and then five of us went out and took shits on the car's bumpers. Then, it was *really* a shitty car, and we sat in our cabin, drinking beer and laughing while the couple cursed at whoever would have been mean enough to make such a mess on their car. Well, that would teach them the danger in coming to cheap cabins at Loon Lake. As I grew older, the malice grew worse. I was 20 years old when we starting playing "polo" by driving the wrong way on one-way streets and smashing headlights with tire-irons. I was 22 when we took the wino, threatened to kill him, and then dumped him in the Arboretum in Seattle. We called all this shit "pranks," but we knew what it was: payback on our part for being born into a fucking world that didn't make any sense. We had to lead double lives, respectable by day, demons by night, because our parents and our teachers and our preachers kept telling us and showing us that society was a construct of lies, that what we thought was true wasn't, and that our worst fears were the actual world. The horse-cock pervert in the Eagles' men's room wasn't an aberration; he was the unvarnished, fucking truth about society. He was Ross's dad with his three-piece suit off. Every goddamn minister or bishop or prelate was just Pastor Fuzz all over again. My father made fun of the stupid people he sold insurance to. I made fun of him because I thought he was a cruel, illiterate prick. If you could, you hurt people somehow, and then made fun of them. Ross and I spent months on a prank. We would call the phone number Glenwood 3333, and then ask if this was "Gwenwood, fwee, fwee, fwee, fwee." When the answer was yes, we would say "Then, let's play dictaphone." The person on the other end would say "What?" And we would say: "Dictaphone up your ass!" and laugh and hang up. It only really worked once, but we were so excited by doing it that we went on and on. We called every five minutes, counting how long it took the man or woman who answered to hang up. We looked up the name of the person who had that phone number. We called and asked for him by name, when he got on the phone, we started the whole thing again: "Is this Gwenwood . . . ?" We called and talked to him using his first name: "George?" "Yes." "Is this Gwenwood . . . ?" We talked to his wife, using her first name. After awhile, they realized that just hanging up wouldn't work. He started swearing at us. That didn't work. We kept calling and calling. Finally, we reduced him to tears and begging. "Please, boys," he said, "please. You're making my wife sick. Please!" "Dictaphone . . . " We stopped calling him after we got bored with the prank; after we figured we had broken the poor fuck. Deprived by law and society of the freedom to kill at random, that was the kind of thing that Western boyos did for fun. It was better when we were older and had cars; then you could see the faces of the people you hurt.

Larry was very short. Most of us were long, gangly Scandinavian types with big shoulders, hands and feet. One of my girlfriends' fathers said that I couldn't enter a door without banging into both sides of the jam. He called me "The Goof;" he called Larry "Midge." Larry measured about five feet three inches tall, but, "Midge" or not, he was mighty tough. He was fast and strong and he liked nothing better than taking on one of the gangly geeks he found around him. We thought it was fun to set up fights for him. We would find some solitary tall guy who we didn't know in the halls of Lewis and Clark. If he was opening his locker, one of us would bump and grab the back of his head and drive him full-face into the locker. He would turn around, fury on his face, and demand to know who did it. Larry would say that it was him. The guy would swing at Larry. Larry would dodge the punch and proceed to pile-drive the guy into his locker with punches that were as fast as a professional boxer. Tight little fights like that were best for Larry, he was so small and so strong that he could beat somebody up by being inside of the other guy's punching range. It must have been like having a little animal attack you, he would be all over the other guy's ribs and stomach and the guy would be futilely swatting at him and swinging right over him. Free-range outdoor fights were a little more risky for Larry. In fact, his last teen-age fight was a late night front yard battle where Larry ended up with a broken collarbone. But, the one fight I will always remember was at Comstock Pool. Larry's opponent was about 6'3" and over two hundred pounds. Larry weighed a maximum of 120. The guy was furious because Larry called him a "fat queer" in front of his girlfriend. The guy swung at Larry and missed. He kept swinging and cursing Larry out and missing as Larry danced around in front of him. Finally Larry did a series of karate leaps and kicked the guy in balls five times. With the fifth kick the guy really doubled up and Larry pushed him backward into the pool. Larry turned to the guy's girlfriend and said: "Fat queers shouldn't fight." After the broken collarbone, Larry got stupid. He hooked up with a guy who did deliveries for Rosauer's market. They stole cases of beer that the guy would leave on the loading dock and that Larry, broken collar-bone cast and all, would pick up and load into his car. They stole about a hundred cases which they blackmarketed to kids they knew. When they got caught, Larry got kicked out of school and was given the choice between the army and jail. He was eighteen and he knew that it was over for him in Spokane. He chose the army. The guy who worked at Rosauer's came from what my father called a "prominent family," so he was fired and fined and went to college in the fall at the University of Arizona. He sent letters back to those of us still in Spokane, where he talked about trips to Nogales—"lots of fucking"—and signed his name with a drawing of a dripping prick. We showed one of the letters to the girlfriend he had left behind, and she broke off with him the same day over the phone. We never saw or heard from Larry again. Larry never had a girlfriend in Spokane. Everybody he might have wanted to go out with thought he was too short. I never liked the guy who went to the University of Arizona. He was the one who sat in his car in my driveway when I was just sixteen and kept sniffing his middle finger and saying "I really love Marty" over and over. I knew what finger-fucking was, but I had never done it, and the smirk on his face made me want to hit him. He was the kind of cowboy I could do without.

We all wanted to fuck "regular girls." Our girlfriends. Whores were wonderful once we discovered them, but like any young mountain men who get the sniff of the perfume of civilization, we wanted the girls whose breasts we could feel in the darkness of our cars to open their legs and invite us in. It didn't happen. Not then. Not in high school. It was all Doris Day fantasy. The guys who did "score" big-talked about it. Lied, exaggerated, showed off rubbers in their wallets. When we looked at their girlfriends, we couldn't imagine ever kissing them because they had had some guy's cock in their mouths. They became whores, sluts. If a guy said that a girl fucked him, then we knew that we could fuck her too, but, as was the whorehouse ethic, we wouldn't kiss her. She could blow us and we would fuck her, but that was it. Once a girl fucked in the sad little, phony, preacher and teacher and businessman society that we lived in, she became no more than a hole. We understood the duplicity and the bullshit of it all, but we were raised to believe in the code of the schoolmarm West, even though we lived right on the fucking frontier. We wanted to fuck "nice girls" like our forefathers had wanted to kill Indians. Make it all meaningless and ours.

When I was five, I read the Classic Comics version of *The Last of the Mohicans*. It affected me in much the same way as *Peter Pan*. I wanted so much to be Natty Bummpo. I wanted an Indian friend like Chingachgook. I was furious with the death of Uncas. I hated the bad Indians more than I loved the good ones. I thought that it was possible for men like Bummpo—the Deerslayer, the Pathfinder—to live in my West. I saw Bummpo and his Indian friends as magic people. They knew the woods and the land so well that they were parts of nature, not separated from it and living in little towns and wearing hats and suits to work in buildings. I thought of my grandfather as the Pathfinder, as Leatherstocking. And I would be Uncas, but I would never die. I went from the comic book to Cooper's novel, then to his other Leatherstocking novels. I forced myself to adore them, but none of them ever equaled the pure realized beauty of the Classic Comic. There I could see it all. The woods of the comic were alive for me, just as the woods around Cathcart would be. I belonged there, amidst the odors of cedar and pine, walking barefoot on the needles of the forest floor. I didn't understand, nor did I need to understand that Cooper's tales took place in forests quite different from the ones I was learning about-the harsh pine and fir woods around Spokane and the lush rainforests on the west side of the Cascades—all I knew was that the woods, the Indians and the animals were all part of the West, my West. I also knew, from the comic book first of all, that Bumppo, or Deerslayer, or Pathfinder, or Leatherstocking or whatever name he went by was by choice a denizen of nature, not a resident of society. His Indian friends were not welcome in white society; he chose to stay with them. I would have to. I would have chosen the life of an outsider. If I give myself time or the drift to *really* think about my life and the world I live in, I will always choose the life of the outsider. Huck Finn and Jim; Ruthie and Sylvie from Marilynne Robinson's *Housekeeping*; Wolverine and Gambit from the *X-Men* comics. I choose those outsiders who love and are able to love. Jim loved Huck and Huck discovered that he loved Jim. When Huck did that, he flashed a hard and permanent good-bye to society. Ruthie loved her Aunt Sylvie and Sylvie loved her. They could not accept the rules of a town. Wolverine held within his small body the potential for terrible violence. He had the weapons of strength, adamantine claws and a magical healing system. He could kill. Instead he loved Jean Grey and served as friend and protector to Kitty Pryde and Jubilation Lee. Gambit was a rogue, a thief. He loved and was loved by Rogue. I hated Tom Sawyer. I felt sorry for Ruthie's sister, Lucille. Superman was adored by humans; Batman depended upon his "secret" identity, and, like Green Arrow and the original Human Torch, had a young boy for his partner. Scott Summers, although he was the leader of the X-Men, was too much of a goody-two-shoes for me. I needed someone who was on the outside, connected to life by love and the kind of responsibility that love brings with it. Those fictional heroes who were doing conscious good or felt a general social obligation were too much like the town settlers I found myself detesting in all the Western stories I read and the Western life I was living. In their righteousness, they became self-righteous, and displaced the very people whose survival they should be protecting; they ended up as part of the nature-destroying evil—Indian Killers!

Oh, what the fuck am I thinking about? What's all this hero crap? It reminds me of when I was drunk and playing Ahab to a auditorium-size class; calling them "my Pequod," and, faking a wooden peg for a leg, stumping around the perimeters of the classroom and up and down the aisles, railing at the poor, frightened or disinterested students. I was never any version of Ahab. Not even drunk. Just a poor, bad actor's imitation of the true rage of a God and Nature defier. No, in all the stuff I've read, if there was ever anyone who I might have looked at and felt a mirror shock, it would have been always and ever Ishmael, the lover of a savage and victim of a brute. Knowing nothing, able only to ask questions and stand in amazement at the wonders of the world; longing ever and only for a transcendental leap from the mast of the Pequod to the ethereal arms of Queeg-Queeg. A scared and none too bright young man who couldn't find a place for himself in society and instead found himself orphaned in the vast sea of nature with only his story to sustain him. I, too, know nothing, am sure of nothing. I see what I see. But when I look at trees, or Coeur d'Alene Lake, or the ocean, or another human being, I am overcome by my own stupidity. If I could only truly be like Ishmael and let what is, be, without feeling the need to question it, then there wouldn't be all this craziness. Ishmael was an Indian Lover. Was my father? When he sold them insurance was he doing it out of love? All my life I've figured he did it as a cheap con, to get money from people who had no real idea of what he was talking about. It does no good to even bother with it now, because the poor bastard's dead as are all the Indians he sold insurance to. Did they think that the insurance meant that they would live forever? Were they that naive as to what the White Man was about? No. But I'm stupid enough to think about something like that. Oh, God! I want so much to know something about the real world! I want so much to put my body and my mind to rest in nature. I don't want to die, but I want to feel the cool peace of wholeness and not feel so fractured, so like a living car spinning around and around, out of control. Brian Wilson wrote a song called "Help me, Rhonda," and I find myself chanting "Help me, Rhonda," like a mantra. At times I say it over and over as though it were the alpha and omega of my psychic world. Help me, Rhonda!

Part of this is real and part of it is imaginary, but it feels so right just to think it. If I, or one, walk by a stream in the forest—not on the banks, in the woods, but close enough that the sound of the stream fills my ears—barefoot, arms out in front of me. Then I can close my eyes and walk through the forest guided by what I hear: the stream, the sounds of birds, the scratching of small animals scurrying through the brush, the buzz of insects. I can feel the forest floor with my feet, so I will not trip. With my arms stretched out in front of me, my fingers will feel any tree or low-hanging branch before I run into it. I am sure that, were I to do this enough, that I would not need my arms held out, that I would be able to hear the trees as I approached them. Then I would be alive in nature. A part of the natural world. I could open my eyes as I chose, to take in the visual part of the beauty I was hearing and smelling, then close them again and be utterly content. I *have* done this. I have closed my eyes and walked in the woods; I have walked in the woods at night, when there were no stars or moon to offer any light. But just for seconds, not minutes, not hours. It was like doing something dangerous on a dare. If it were a pitch-black night, I would quickly turn on my flashlight; if it were day, I would open my eyes after a few tentative steps. So. I wonder if I could live that way, as a creature of the forest. It would be wonderful, if it only weren't too late. But, of course, it is.

* * *

Stop.

* * *

What I'm thinking about is the future. Having a future. What about stopping time—my time—now? No. Not letting the fire go out and freezing and starving to death in this cabin; and not walking out into the snow and onto the lake until I reach the end of the ice and step over. What if I set as a goal for myself the same goal my Swedish ancestors had. Struggle out of the snow and the woods and over the mountains to the shore of the sea. Say I could get to the furthest Pacific beach on the coast of

Vancouver Island, and that once there I could walk down from the woods onto the flat breadth of the hard sand beach. It would be at night and I would hear nothing save the breaking of the waves in the surf and occasional night-cries of gulls and shore birds; I would see nothing save for the star-filled sky and the moon and the moon's light glistening on the water. I could walk out into the water and drop to my knees letting the waves break across my chest and face and then let go and . . . be gone. The idea of that kind of peace starts a soft humming in my head. I don't want to think anymore. Everything is so hard to do. Even remembering. All of it. The confusion, the anger, the sorrow, the regret. It's all in the past. It's all in my memory. I don't even know if I remember correctly. I don't know if I saw or experienced what I remember, or if I am just making it up. Has my life been real, or just some story that I am constantly in the process of telling? Telling a story with no audience save for myself. That's what Ishmael did. What do I know? What can I say that is absolutely true and real? I am alone now. I am in a cabin on Coeur d'Alene Lake in Northern Idaho, in the middle of winter, with very little food and water, and no idea whatsoever of how to leave here and get back to civilization. That much is true. That much I know. I am tired. If I go to sleep, I am afraid that I will die. Yet if I stay awake, all I will do is think. I will either remember, or I will run in the jungle of abstracts, trying to figure out if there is a difference between right and wrong, or if there even are such things as right and wrong; I will try to peg my memories of my experiences to whatever I think right and wrong might be, and I will end up driving myself crazy. I will be some fool crouching in the corner, too confused to eat or drink. Maybe I'll start to scream, not in the hope that someone will hear me, but just to stop the explosions in my head. Thinking this way is not pretty; it is not good. I have to find a way to stop the words in my head. I don't want to make any more comments to myself. I'm getting to the point I was at when I yelled, "Gilkey," and didn't know what to say or why I had yelled at her, so I said "God, you're a whore." No connections between the words my brain makes come out into the world and any sort of reality. If I could just see things in my memory now, not comment, just look, as though I were simply observing things in the world outside my mind. I think that's the way animals live. They observe through their senses and then act or re-act according to what they see. Even if they spoke, they would not say, "God, you're a whore," because they would feel no obligation to say something out of the embarrassment of not knowing what to say. No awkward social situations: See, smell, fight or lick. That's the idea. In my mind, see everyone, smell everyone, hear everyone, then fight or lick. But don't goddamn think about it!

* * *

Now I'm sober. So simple. No shakes, no crazy guilt, no visions. Just back there. Where it all began. Back with the pain. I can't scream anymore, because it's all real and solid. Oh, my, what a fucked-up way to live! The reality of sobriety just happened to me. Now the thinking is gone. I can't even remember what I was thinking about. My father, I guess. I don't know for sure. I don't think it was my wives or my children or my brother or my cousins or my aunts and uncles, or even my long dead mother. And, I don't even think I was really thinking about myself. It must have been my father, and what a bastard he was to the world that held him when he died. How much hate that miserable son of a bitch had in him. He hated so much that he couldn't even say good-bye. He just gasped out. Alone. All of which was probably just the way he wanted it. Who am I to judge? Who the fuck am I? I'm not exactly an example of human love perfected—there's barely a shred of it in my heart or mind. I have pretty well—and I'm speaking as a sober man here—fucked up everything and everyone I've touched. No big deal. No one seriously hurt, but there are reasons for everything. So, I sit in this goddamn cabin in a Coeur d'Alene winter and cry for the stupidity of my dead father. Well, I said another stupid thing. Thank God that I'm only talking to myself. Saying that there are reasons for everything is no more than a hiss of steam coming out of one of those New York City pavement grates. I say everything is simple and I'm sober and I'm not thinking anymore, and all that I am doing is setting up one more self-conscious, pretentious dodge: Always the actor. I can't trust myself. The more I say that I'm not thinking, the more I am. I . . . I . . . I . . . I fucking I. Over and over. I'm listening to myself trying to talk fast about nothing, and my voice echoes in my head, mocking me. Why do I hate my father? Because he didn't love me. Who did? I don't know. There was a whore one time, in Priest River, who told me that she fucked anybody who had five dollars so that her little sister wouldn't have to; she could go to college. I remember saying at the time—I was seventeen—that maybe her sister would want to do just what she did, fuck anybody who wanted her and that I couldn't see anything wrong with that. Then she cried. I don't think that my Aunt Mina would ever have cried about something like that.

My mother would have; my father would have cursed; but Mina might have said, "Maybe you're right. Nobody should ever be sure about anything that another person might do or want." Something like that. That's also Crazy Horse thinking. At least the way I want to think about him. Sad, stupid drunk Cowboys can spend their quiet hours alone grieving over who loved them and who didn't, who hurt them and who they hurt. In the lonely West, they can kill themselves by thinking. Hunters, herders, archetypal lonely men, they really have nothing to think about but themselves. My father was like that. Lonely. That word haunts my mind. I say that cowboys are lonely, riding after things in a world that is too big for them. And then I say my father was lonely, working, fighting, achieving in the little tribe he called his city, his hometown, Spokane. At the rock bottom of all of it, is the Mountain Man, when he comes, like the bear, out of his winter cave to face the springtime, any different from the insurance salesman in the town taking off his galoshes and the snow-tires off his car to face the rainy spring road of sales? No. No. No. They all—Mountain Man, father, grandfather—wanted the same thing. And so do I. There is something in all of us that would stand apart from the snarl of the angered, frightened grizzly facing a gun or a cougar in the woods; something that would like to look at the creatures of nature as our partners in living. No more beasts to be shot for sport; no more niggers; no more chinks; no more redskins; no more wetbacks. We don't want to be animals that make each other wild. We want to live in peace in the world. We want to be like what we think Indians are and were. Just saying that to myself sounds stupid. It isn't Indians, it is the quality of harmony: sounding a note with your voice in the woods or on the city street and feeling the resonant hum of creation joining you. I say that for all of us, knowing full well what I have done to fight that harmony and imagining what others have done. I say that we really didn't want to do any of it. We're sorry.

And I am tired deep down in my heart. It's so strange to say that I am speaking for everyone, when I can barely form any words at all in my own mind. The word love sticks somehow on an invisible tongue somewhere in my brain, and I stammer and stammer and words choke me. I have no ideas anymore. I don't know if I ever did. I only know that I am in a place of the senses. I see, hear, taste, smell and feel. I want that to be enough for me. When I think, it is only of the past, and there, in that vast tangle of events, people and emotions, memories of joy are overwhelmed by instant terrors. I am a Westerner, ruled by fear, constantly trying to dodge the realization of my own insignificance. I know that, as a drunk, I want to feel myself powerful and in control of my universe, but as I sober up I realize that I am unable to create a universe that would hold me precious at its center. So, I stand small and frightened, no man to match any mountain. I know nothing of the future. I can not imagine the future. I seem stranded in the present as though it were a still moment in time, one that I have created so that I could make the life that I have lived live once more, in a memory that cannot distinguish between fact and fantasy.

What do I do now?

Well, mirabile dictu, deus ex machina, I hear the dog at the door to the cabin, scratching to get in. Does he have some kind of fucking answer for me? I'll open the door and find out.

"Well, dog, dog, dog, Crazy Horse, have you news for me from the world of the lake? Have you come to . . . ?"

The dog seemed to explode in front of me, on the threshold of the door. There was a cloud of steam in the cold blowing in from outside. And then . . . it was . . . he was . . . him. The dead Indian from Trent Alley. Only now I could see his eyes. He was looking straight into my face. His eyes were the dog's; they were Mina's whore's eyes; beautiful, magic eyes.

"You expected me, didn't you," he said in a soft, lyrical voice.

"Yes. But . . . "
"Different."
"Yes."
"You stole my hat. That was not good."
"I'm sorry. I . . . didn't know . . . "
"There is much you don't know."

We looked at each other.

"Well," he said, "you asked for me. Are you ready?"

His eyes were pulling at me. Daring me to go deeper. "Ready for what?"

"To go."
"Where?"
"Home."
"Where is it?'
"We'll find out. Are you ready?"
"Yes."